THE MASK SHOP OF DOCTOR BLAACK

THE MASK SHOP OF DOCTOR BLAACK

STEVE RASNIC TEM

HEX PUBLISHERS

THE MASK SHOP OF DOCTOR BLAACK

Developmental edits by Mario Acevedo
Copyedits by Jennifer Melzer and Dean Wyant
Cover art and design by Kirk DouPonce
Art direction by Joshua Viola
Illustrations by Aaron Lovett
Typesets and formatting by Dustin Carpenter

A Hex Publishers Book

Published & Distributed by Hex Publishers, LLC
PO BOX 298
Erie, CO 80516

www.HexPublishers.com

Hex Publishers TM is a trademark of Hex Publishers, LLC.
Joshua Viola, Publisher

Hardcover ISBN-13: 978-0-9997736-0-4
Paperback ISBN-13: 978-0-9997736-1-1
Ebook ISBN-13: 978-0-9997736-2-8

First Hex Edition: September 2018
10 9 8 7 6 5 4 3 2 1

Printed in the U.S.A.

For my children, both kids and grandkids.

*L*eaves *like a scatter of colored glass, air so cold she thought it would freeze the trees and make them break, but then the sun would come out, and all those pieces of color began to glow and set fire to her heart.*

Fall was Laura's favorite time of year, with the leaves changing colors and the light coming through her bedroom window with that soft, warm, golden color that always made her smile, and the air smelling just a little bit like smoke, like the world was cooking up something hot and sweet and spicy.

This year autumn was even more special because

the summer had been so hot and long and miserable. Everybody in her family had been affected by the heat except her little brother Trevor, the maniac, who always had to be different. He just ran around in his swimming trunks all day, jumping in and out of his wading pool.

Her usually calm and confident dad came home from the office every day looking exhausted with big wet patches under his arms. And Laura didn't know if it was heatstroke or not but her mom had suddenly turned into this crazy cleaning lady, always washing dishes or polishing something or straightening or rearranging something or down on the floor on her hands and knees wiping and scrubbing and scraping.

One afternoon Laura came into the kitchen and saw her mother just standing there, staring out the window with her hands in the dishwater, not moving for so long Laura was a little afraid. Then her mom said quietly, "I guess it's a good thing your granddad didn't have to deal with this heat wave. He never managed hot days well, not even back when I was your age."

Granddad died early in the spring, and that made this summer the most difficult summer Laura could remember. Because there had been no movies out with Granddad, or trips to the lake with Granddad, or sitting

out on the porch swing while he asked her what she'd
been doing with her time and what she dreamed about
for her future.

She'd never met anyone else like him. She didn't
think she ever would. The fact that he was gone, it was
like saying the moon was gone from the sky. She could
hardly believe it.

Trevor worried if it stayed that hot maybe they'd
have to cancel Halloween because whoever heard of a
hot Halloween?

"They'd still have it, Trevor," she told him. "It's
just that everybody would go trick-or-treating in their
swimsuits."

After school one day she was sitting in her room.
The window was open and there was a branch of the
old Maple so close to her window she could touch it.
She grabbed the tip of it and pulled until the branch
was inside her room.

By dinnertime she had used her watercolors to paint
as many Maple leaves as she could reach. When she was
done they didn't look like any Autumn leaves she had
ever seen before because she had added so much pink,
and blue, and violet—but that was okay with her. She
knew the next little rain would wash all the colors off,

but she didn't mind. The things she imagined rarely lasted long.

Then one day there was this little mischievous wind that wandered through the streets as if lost, picking up trash, dropping it and then picking it up again, going up onto people's porches and ringing wind chimes, shaking the trees a few seconds, then going to the next house, visiting every house on the block before running away to play its joke somewhere else.

The next day she noticed that the leaves were beginning to change color. After a couple more weeks leaves were falling everywhere. Along the edges of the street, just after the sun came up, were little piles of orange and yellow and red leaves. Sometimes after a light rain the sun reflected off the wet leaves and they looked like piles of precious coins just waiting for Laura to pick up.

October came, and the browns and yellows and oranges of the late afternoon sky matched the nuts and bananas and oranges her mom put out in a bowl on the dining room table. The houses glowed like they were burning inside. Her mother made lots of pies, hot soups, cinnamon teas, brownies, and candied apples. Even Trevor seemed satisfied.

*I*n the big stores downtown: bright displays of glowing green and orange and red against deep black backgrounds in the windows. Haunted houses and Frankenstein and Dracula statues of all sizes, gray Styrofoam tombstones, orange plastic pumpkins overflowing with treats. Plastic masks of every cartoon character she'd ever heard of, every actor, every hero anyone ever wanted to be, hanging from the back wall. Piles of thin cloth dresses with skeleton prints, snake prints, monkey prints, superhero prints. A long winding row of overlapping vampire fangs looking like a snake skeleton. Inside the stores the kids were tearing the cheaply-made costumes off the racks, masks and belts and accessories flying everywhere, getting stepped on, getting dirty, *getting broken. Kids crying because they couldn't find the right size, or the costume they wanted, or one with all its parts. Moms and Dads just stood there, looking at their watches, afraid to get too close, afraid they'd get shoved out of the way, trampled, their own clothes torn. Every once in a while one of them screamed at their kid, saying it's time to go, but nobody could hear them.*

This year was going to be Laura's last for trick-or-treating. Last year was supposed to be her last, but Laura's parents said Trevor wasn't ready to go out by himself quite yet, so they decided for her that she had to go with him. And she had to wear a costume so that, as their mother said, "He won't feel too self-conscious," which was ridiculous, but Mom wouldn't listen to reason. Appearing in costume at a party, or in a play, performing in a costume, that was one thing—Laura liked all that. But trick-or-treating? That was kid stuff.

"Mom, I'm just way too old to be out there in costume, going door to door, begging."

"Begging? Oh, Laura, you can be so dramatic."

"Well, maybe it isn't begging but it feels pretty close. What about the party? You said I could go." She'd been invited to a Halloween party one of the other parents was throwing, just for the kids in her class. Just for people her age.

"I said *probably* you could go, but only after Trevor is done with his trick or treating. I thought you liked Halloween."

Laura sat and stewed, but didn't say anything. Her mother kept working on dinner and didn't look up. It was how they kept the peace. Laura knew when she was getting angry and shouldn't talk—she might say something she didn't really mean. And her mother knew not to look at Laura when she knew Laura was mad—that always irritated both of them.

Of course it was going to be all about the treating—her parents wouldn't be too happy if they played any tricks, not that Laura would. Still, every year their Dad said "No tricks!" as they went out the door. And he'd laugh like it was some great joke he'd just thought up for the very first time.

Trevor was going to get to decide when he'd had enough trick-or-treating. Knowing Trevor, that probably meant four hours and six bags full of treats she'd have to help him carry. They'd need a wheelbarrow for all his treats! No way was she going to get to that party.

No way was that fair, but obviously there was nothing she could do about it.

After all that time talking, or not-talking, to her mother, Laura was worn out. She struggled up the stairs. Usually she liked to race up the stairs. Tonight it felt like climbing a mountain. On her way to her bedroom she stopped in the hall outside Grandad's old room. Laura used to visit Grandad in his room nearly every day until he died. She sometimes went in there after he died, too, to look around and remember him.

Laura eased open the door to Grandad's room and slipped inside. Her parents never told her not to go in there, but she never asked, afraid they might say no. She turned on the light, hoping it would be just like it had been before, but she already knew it wouldn't be.

Some of Grandad's things were still in the room— his dresser and sitting chair, and a few of his old pictures— but they'd been crowded into one corner. It was like her mom had started to move them out, but couldn't quite make herself go all the way. Her mom had taken over the rest of the room, however, with her sewing machine and a bookcase and her scrapbooking table. There was also a small radio so she could listen to some of her favorite music—syrupy, romantic songs sung mostly by female singers.

Laura didn't think her mother had done anything wrong by moving stuff into Grandad's old room like that—she deserved her own place to get away to just like everybody else in the family. It seemed like she was always doing things for everybody and people didn't appreciate it enough.

But it still felt bad. It felt unfair that one day Grandad was there and the next day he wasn't and the rest of the family was supposed to go on like there was nothing missing. If something happened to Laura what would they do to her room, turn it into a laundry room or something? What did it mean that you could be so important in other people's daily lives and then not be important at all?

Later, when she was by herself in her room, Laura worked herself up until she was crying over how unfair everything was. She kept thinking about what her mother said to her, "I thought you liked Halloween." Well, of course she did! She even secretly wanted to go trick or treating one last time, just not with a little kid. Her mother didn't understand the first thing about her. She pulled her pillow over her head and cried.

Trevor wasn't so bad, actually—a little goofy of course, but really not so bad. Sometimes she wanted to chop him into little pieces and flush him down the toilet, but her dad said it was pretty normal for her to think that way. She could think terrible things like that sometimes because she loved him. Trevor had been really sick when he was about three years old, and had spent a lot of time in the hospital. He made it through that awful time, but he was still smaller than most of the boys his age, on the skinny side, and kind of pale. So if he looked a little goofy he had a pretty good excuse. Some kids at school called Trevor "The Ghost," but not when Laura was around. He was lucky to still be alive. She was lucky he was still alive. The whole family was.

Now, if she could just make it through this one last Halloween without him annoying her half to death, things would be great.

L *ittle kids ran around in hard plastic masks way too big for their faces—the eye holes too far apart so they could only see out of one eye, making them run into trees and sign posts and each other. Making them whine. Oh, it was so annoying the way they whined! Like a bunch of sick cats. The mouth holes and nose holes were always in the wrong places, too, so they had to keep lifting up their masks so they could breathe. Running, running, then lifting their masks panting and gasping, whining, smelling of sweat and candy.*

Trevor didn't want a cheap costume from one of those stores in the mall, or from one of those big discount stores crawling with hundreds of crazy kids. He didn't want one of those costumes with a mask that didn't fit, that left you out of breath by the time you got to people's front doors. He didn't want one of those cheap costumes that tore up the back and split across the belly five minutes after you first put it on, like it was made out of colored tissue paper instead of cloth.

For once Laura agreed with the weird little guy. She didn't want her own very last Halloween costume to be tacky and poorly-made. It should be something special.

"We need something special!" Trevor shouted.

"Quite special," Laura agreed, although a little less loudly.

And that's how they decided to make that last minute trip into Doctor Blaack's Mask Shop.

Doctor Blaack's had moved into an empty space in the old downtown mall the previous fall, just before last year's Halloween. A lot of people, including her parents, were surprised. Nobody went to that mall anymore—in fact there were rumors it was going to be torn down.

"What a terrible place to start a business!" her dad said.

Laura thought that was a little mean, but she could certainly see what he meant. The old downtown mall was a shabby little three-block stretch of buildings, mostly empty except for some used book stores, a thrift shop, and an antique store that was never open as far as she could tell. People were used to stores moving out of the old mall, but a store moving in, that was a new and unexpected event. People laughed about it. The new store wasn't a cool, trendy place. The outside of it was dirty and cracked and needed repair just like the rest of those old buildings.

"And that spelling? *Blaack*? No wonder children can't spell," her mother said. "Pretty irresponsible, if you ask me."

"Perhaps that's just the way the man spells his last name, dear. A person can't help the name they're given, unless they live in Hollywood I suppose," her father said over the top edge of his morning paper. He did that a lot on workday mornings. It occurred to Laura that if her father ever went out trick-or-treating, he might go dressed as a newspaper.

"Well, I just believe it's a rather eccentric spelling for a perfectly ordinary color. It's an odd business anyway, don't you think, selling masks? Who needs a mask except at Halloween?"

Laura and Trevor took the city bus downtown the

day before Halloween, right after school. At first the bus was pretty full, but by the second stop half the passengers had left to transfer to other lines. After that they trickled out—three, four, six at a time—people in business suits, hospital workers, high school kids returning to their families' apartments in the tall buildings near the town's center.

By the time Laura and Trevor reached their stop they were almost the only ones left on the bus. An elderly lady sitting near the front climbed out of her seat carrying several shopping bags and headed down the steps toward the door. Laura wondered what she would do if one of the bags ripped open and spilled everything out. That would be really embarrassing. What if there were granny panties in one of those bags?

The only other passenger, a tall, skinny man in a bright blue suit, got out next. He carried a parrot in a cage. Laura waited for that parrot to say something the entire trip, but although it looked like it was about to speak lots of times—its eyes staring at her and its mouth wide open—it never said anything. Now as the man was going down the steps the parrot winked at her. At least that's what it looked like. Maybe it was just an involuntary twitch. But then the man himself turned and winked at her, too. Laura felt completely creeped out.

"Are you kids getting off here?" The bus driver turned around, smiling. Laura didn't like being called a kid but she appreciated the reminder that they were at their stop. No telling where they would've ended up if he hadn't said anything, maybe "the end of the line", which was a place she'd heard about but never seen. In any case it didn't sound like the kind of place you'd visit on purpose. She grabbed Trevor's hand and they scrambled off.

The mall was one block over. They walked as quickly as they could because she wasn't really sure when Doctor Blaack's closed for the day. She hadn't found any ads for the store in the paper—which seemed an odd thing for a costume shop just before Halloween—and odder still that the shop had no phone number listed. Normally Laura would have decided Doctor Blaack's had gone out of business, but one of her school friends, Tommy Jones, insisted he had been down there two days before and bought a mask.

"So what's the store like inside? Is it really, really cool?" Laura had asked, excited.

"Well, I don't know. It's just a store. It's got some neat stuff, I guess. I don't really remember much about it."

"Tommy! You were there just two days ago!" Tommy just shrugged.

The old downtown mall was closed to cars to make it safe for pedestrians. When she was just a little girl, long before Trevor was born, Mom and Dad took her down here for pizza, ice cream, and a movie. The movie theater, *The Paladium*, was still there, but it had been closed a long time. The paint on the front of the building was peeling, leaving big piles of gray and brown and black flakes on the sidewalk out front.

Laura couldn't remember the name of the movie they had seen except that it was kind of exciting, kind of strange, and that it featured dancing hippos, so it must have been some kind of cartoon. She also remembered that she had lost half of her ice cream cone on somebody else's seat, but she hadn't been able to decide how upset she should be because she was already too full to eat anymore.

Now the dimness and the general shabbiness of the old outdoor mall made her sad. Here fall just meant a few spindly trees planted in bare dirt. These trees didn't even have leaves, so she couldn't tell if the trees had gone to sleep for the winter or if they were just dead. The paper and plastic trash blowing through the street made her think of fallen leaves at their ugliest, when they've been on the ground so long they start to rot. Most of the buildings were peeling and flaking as if they were dying, and the low autumn sun hiding on the other side of these buildings made everything look miserable. The spaces between the buildings received no light at all—it made her walk faster because she worried about what might be hiding there.

But halfway down the street she noticed a few lights burning over an old-fashioned hand-painted sign. As they walked closer she could see the fancy black lettering on a blood-red background more clearly: THE MASK SHOP OF DOCTOR BLAACK. The second "A" in "BLAACK" was just a little bit above the rest of the letters, as if it knew it didn't belong.

Surrounding the words themselves the sign had just the craziest bunch of pictures floating in the red: ribbons, and crowns, and flowers, and of course masks, dozens of little masks perched on the letters, hiding inside the "O's," lying flat beneath the huge "B" as if crushed and broken by its weight.

"Those lights are on. Maybe it's open," Laura said.

"You go first," Trevor said behind her.

Laura led the way, but before they reached Doctor Blaack's, with its dark display windows full of even darker shapes, they passed a few empty store windows. They were spray-painted with colorful graffiti that might have been words, but they must have been in some foreign language. Laura stopped for just a second to see if she could understand any of it when she thought she saw something moving deep inside the shadows on the other side of the glass. Something flapping or somebody waving.

"Laura," Trevor whispered. "Why are you stopping?"

"I don't know," she replied. "I thought I saw something." She stepped up to the smeared, shadow-filled window and cupped her hands against it. The glass was freezing cold. She felt Trevor breathing hard behind her. She knew he was nervous—she was too, although she couldn't have explained exactly why. She pressed her nose against the glass and looked in.

It was mostly empty, and looked like it had been for a very long time. A couple of sets of metal shelves lay on their sides in the middle of the floor. Everywhere there was evidence of things torn out of the walls, out of the ceiling. Electrical wires dangled, pipes were exposed.

Wallpaper had been torn out in irregular strips, leaving ragged patterns of bare wall like giant claw marks. Dust covered everything like some thick, furry growing thing, like black moss.

A dirty mound lay on the floor near the back, under the windows. She couldn't tell what it was: a bunch of rags, some leaves, or maybe some dead animal. There were arms and legs lying nearby, twisted into weird positions, piled up next to a couple of torsos, three heads. Parts of dummies. Mannequins, so maybe this had been a clothing store. She hoped so. It would be pretty weird if it wasn't.

Empty stores had always bothered her. They seemed so useless, so unnatural, so wrong. She'd much rather see a store torn down than to see it left empty.

In the back wall of the store she could see through the windows to the river that ran through this part of town. It was hard to believe something so pretty lay just on the other side of that dingy glass and this big dirty room. It must take a lot of dedication, she thought, to run a store, and she wondered if she'd ever have that much dedication for anything.

"Laura. Laura! It's getting late!" Trevor yanked on her arm. She turned around. He looked up at her, obviously worried. "Laura, you're being spacey. I just hate it when you get spacey!"

She couldn't stop herself from smiling. "I'm sorry. I was just thinking. I promise not to be spacey, okay? Let's go get our masks."

*F*_{aces of angels and faces of devils. Faces of witches,}
vampires, werewolves, and mummies. Faces that
weren't really faces at all. Faces of robots, cars, rocket ships,
and even a toaster! A toaster! Cats and dogs and rats and
rabbits, chicks and lizards and bumble bees. Every superhero
face from every comic book she'd ever heard of, every hero
who had ever flown, run, crawled, or moved mountains
with his or her bare hands. All the pretend faces and all the
faces she saw each and every day. And all the hidden, secret
faces she never wanted to see, ever.

Laura estimated there must have been at least a

hundred masks in the window of Doctor Blaack's mask shop, maybe two hundred, maybe even more. But maybe a great deal less. She'd never been very good at guessing numbers of things. It could be beans in a jar, birds in a flock, a pile of Christmas cards on a table, or Halloween masks hung row after row in a huge store window display. It didn't seem to matter what the things were, or how they were placed, she was just never any good at guessing the number of them. She was usually dozens, but sometimes hundreds, wrong. All she could see in her head were "lots." Like now—lots and lots of masks.

Their cousin Roger, on the other hand, had always been excellent at guessing the numbers of things. He'd won a bicycle guessing the number of marbles in an absolutely huge glass jar in the front window of Wilkins' Sporting Goods. He was only two or three marbles off. He was always only two or three off, no matter what he was guessing at. Laura's mother said Roger had a "mathematical mind." Roger was going to be a great scientist one day. Everybody seemed to know that.

Laura had no idea what she was going to be one day. Everybody else she knew seemed to have a plan, or a dream, and some of her friends had those dreams for years. Even Trevor was absolutely certain he was going to be an astronaut one day. That seemed crazy to her, just one of those impossible fantasies kids get into their heads sometimes—like wanting to be a giraffe, or a giant with two heads—but she was still a little jealous that he could be so sure about what he wanted to be.

She didn't understand it—during her short life she'd already changed her mind a half dozen times about important stuff: favorite colors, favorite music, favorite movie actors, favorite things to do on a Saturday afternoon. How could she possibly know what she was going to want, or like, in another ten years? When she asked her mom about it her mom said, "Oh, don't worry so much about it. You'll figure it out." But what if she didn't figure it out? What if she became one of those people with nothing to do, who just walked around all day looking for things to do?

Laura couldn't think of anything she did well, and certainly nothing anybody would ever pay her for. Mom sometimes said that if they paid people to daydream, Laura would be a millionaire. Laura didn't say anything, but she was pretty sure such jobs had to exist. Daydreaming wasn't the only skill you would need, certainly, but maybe it was a start for some special kind of job like writing, painting, acting, film making, music, or fashion design.

If you could dream something up, maybe you could learn to create it as well.

She certainly did have a talent for letting her mind wander. "Laura! Laura, let's go inside! It's getting late!" She gazed down at Trevor yanking on her sleeve.

She glanced around: It *was* getting late. The shadows up and down the mall were larger, deeper, blacker than they had been only a short time before. Pretty soon, she knew, this was going to feel like a very different place.

The light bulbs above the sign for Doctor Blaack's buzzed and blinked and sizzled overhead. They sounded just like Doctor Frankenstein's laboratory in one of those old black and white movies. In the display window the uncountable masks winked and grinned in the spreading shadows. She clutched Trevor's hand so tightly he yelped as she pulled on the doorknob and dragged him inside.

It didn't look like anyone had been in Doctor Blaack's shop for a very long time. The counters were dusty and there were little bits of trash and other debris on the floor. "Hello? Is anyone here?" No one answered, but there were dim lights on in the ceiling and the door had been unlocked. It *had* to be open.

The shelves were crowded and dark, so Laura didn't recognize most of the things that were on them, just that there was a jumble of square and round shapes, short and tall and narrow and wide shapes, painted every color she'd ever seen or imagined, with odd things—springs and strings and large rubber feet and tiny gloved hands and rods and cones and balls and such—hanging out over the edges. Here and there a painted face stared out from a shelf full of shadows, or maybe a furry glove with fingers spread, or a huge jar with scarves hanging out of it, decorated with paintings of eyes. Laura stared at her feet as she crossed the floor. Her white tennis shoes left pale shoeprints in the greasy dust.

"Yuck! This place is filthy!" Trevor said.

"Shhhh…" Laura warned, although she didn't know why she was doing that. The store *was* filthy, maybe the dirtiest place she'd ever been. Small flakes of dust floated down from the ceiling. She could taste the mustiness of it, the grit scratching away at her tongue.

Their shoes made no sound as they walked down the narrow aisle lined with old counters on one side of the store, toward an even larger counter at the back. The thick dirt made the floor feel soft and mushy.

"Gee, look at all the masks," Trevor whispered behind her.

You can say that again, she thought, although what she really wanted right now was for her little brother to be quiet. Masks hung from the shelves that towered against the wall. Masks were stacked in high piles on the gray glass counter-tops. Hundreds, maybe thousands, of masks lay in wide bins like an avalanche of faces. And high above her head gleaming wire zig-zagged from wall to wall, masks hanging from clothespins as if someone had washed them and hung them up to dry.

She had never seen so many masks in one place before. Anteaters and bears and clowns and dogs and elephants and furry things by the score. Ghosts and heroes and icemen with jagged teeth and bad guys' eyes and lopsided noses and murderers' mouths. Enough masks for everybody in town, enough masks for two Halloweens! Maybe even three! But something was wrong...

"Boy! How you gonna choose just one?" Trevor cried. "These are the neatest masks I ever saw!"

So many of the masks appeared to be staring at her. With animal eyes and evil eyes, eyes that were white circles and eyes that were deep black holes.

"So which one you gonna choose, Laura? Which one? Want me to help you choose? I can help you choose. I'd be *glad* to help you *choose!*"

Oh, put a sock in it! she thought fiercely. But what she actually said was, "That's okay. I can choose. Thanks anyway."

They never made it to that big counter. They walked and they walked and then it just wasn't there. Laura couldn't figure out what move they'd made to get to where they were, but suddenly they were standing in a skinny aisle that divided a sea of costumes: masks and shirts and pants and masks and dresses hanging on wires dangling from the ceiling, masks on mannequins standing like soldiers at attention, masks lined up in rows and piled to the ceiling.

Some of them appeared to be the cheap plastic masks you could buy in any store, but there were just a few of those, thrown into little bins under a *BARGAIN* sign. Most of Doctor Blaack's masks were far fancier, constructed out of rubber and cloth and hair, molded into every line and curve and shape and expression she could imagine a face might be capable of, and so real it was majorly creepy the way they stared at her, ready to move, to jump or jabber or sing, but not doing anything at the moment because she was looking at them.

She spun around, trying to take it all in. Between the costumes hanging and costumes standing, beyond the wobbly stacks of boxes, Laura could see even more masks and costumes and parts of costumes hanging on another distant wall, displayed on shelves, falling out onto the floor.

Suddenly she began to panic. She grabbed onto Trevor's hand to protect him, but she was the one who was feeling scared. She felt like she might suffocate. There was just *too much stuff* jammed into this little store! The air was full of dust and well, costumes! An avalanche of costumes! And so dark! Stores weren't supposed to be so dark! Laura couldn't even recognize most of the faces on the masks it was so dark. There was a blue spotlight directly overhead, but that didn't really help her see any better. It just creeped her out more.

She noticed that there was a little bit of light coming up from the floor. She crouched down and looked around under all the hanging costumes. There were lights attached to the floor boards, the little lights you sometimes saw marking the aisle of an airplane or a movie theater. But the paths these lights appeared to be marking went off in several different directions, crossing and re-crossing each other like spider webs until it made her dizzy trying to figure them out.

This had to be the unfriendliest, least helpful store Laura had ever been in. How were you supposed to find anything? And if you didn't know what you were looking for, how were you supposed to choose? She didn't even see any price tags on anything. And where were all the sales clerks? Usually when you walked into a store they came running from all directions eager for your business.

Then between two enormous witch costumes—the kind of outfits two eight-hundred-pound witches might wear—she saw the large counter again in the distance, at the back of the store, and there was a cash register on it!

"Trevor," she said. "Pick a mask—let's get out of here."

"You first," he replied with a shaky voice. "You wanted a mask, too, Laura."

"Okay, okay." She tried to focus on individual masks, but it was hard. Having so many of them together, so many pairs of eyes, so many noses and ears and mouths and chins, they weren't just masks anymore, they weren't just make-believe. It was as if hundreds, or even thousands of faces were spread out in front of you, staring at you, watching your every move. And you had no idea what was going on behind those faces, what they were thinking. They weren't all human, after all. Well, she thought, *none* of them were human, actually. Even so, you could make up a human being's thoughts, you could imagine that. But all these other creatures? Lions and tigers and bears, oh my!

She'd never much liked wearing masks, anyway. They were hard to breathe through and they made her face hot and damp, and they always smelled funny inside, like an old tennis shoe on a hot day or the lunch in your locker you forgot about until one day you smelled it. Most Halloweens Laura had just used pretty make-up, and then she would go out as a princess or a fairy queen or a cheerleader or something feminine like that. Something all girly-girl. And she wasn't that girly-girl in real life, at least she didn't think so, so those were pretty good disguises for somebody like her.

But this year she didn't really want anyone to know it was her, that she, Miss Laura Who-Was-Finally-Supposed-to-Be-Maturing, was still going trick or treating. She'd just die if anybody recognized her. This year, she *had* to wear a mask. But what kind? This store had pretty much every kind of creature you could think of, and creatures you could never have thought of, not in a million years. Anything with fur, scales, feathers, wings, or antennae. Anything that crawled, slithered, stumbled, or flew.

Laura began studying the masks that looked gruesome. Many of the masks in Doctor Blaack's were on the gruesome side. Hideous witches and mutated animals and faces with three eyes or with a nose or ear torn off. Sometimes the faces had a nail or a knife or an axe sticking out of them with fake blood oozing down. Like these creatures walked around like that all day. Like they went grocery shopping or to a movie like that.

One mask had a face like a monkey's but with the wide open eyes of a fish and long bright feathers growing out of its cheeks. One mask was like a mirror—when you looked into that face what stared back was your own face. Another mask was so dark Laura couldn't tell exactly what its face looked like, but when you stared at it long enough it felt like the darkest, blackest, deepest hole you'd ever looked into, and if you fell into that hole you'd fall forever.

"Ohhhh, Laura! Those masks are *too scary*. I couldn't look at a mirror if I wore one of *those* masks!"

"You don't *have* to get a gruesome mask. There are *lots* to choose from."

"Look at all these masks! Must be a billion of 'em!"

"A few hundred, Trevor. Maybe a thousand," Laura said. "Just pick one, okay? I'll pick one, you'll pick one, then we'll be out of here." She just wanted to get to that distant counter, buy some silly mask, and leave. But for some reason the counter looked to be even farther away than the last time she'd looked.

She stopped and rubbed her eyes, but that didn't help at all. The counter still looked miles away. *You're being silly*, she told herself. She looked around for Trevor but couldn't find him. She felt herself beginning to panic again. She could hardly breathe. *Where was he?*

She looked back at the mirror mask and the monkey fish mask and they, too, were now miles away. She felt as if she were shrinking. The aisle she stood in went on and on until it disappeared into the darkest dark she could imagine.

The costumes hanging on each side of her seemed to move closer every time she breathed in, as if she were sucking them toward her. She considered holding her breath so that they wouldn't get any closer, but she knew she couldn't hold her breath for very long. The edges of the ceiling seemed to be bending down toward her. Any second she expected the things on the top shelves to fall off and crash down on her head. She tried to move further away from the shelves and got completely tangled up in the hanging costumes.

She turned and looked for the counter again and now it was so far away it was as if she were looking at it through the wrong end of a telescope. It looked so tiny she could have put it into a match box.

"Laura! Look at this!"

Laura turned toward Trevor's voice. A bright red tongue yards long licked at her face. When she brushed it away two huge buggy eyes dangled from the ends of their long, pale stems in front of her nose.

Laura screamed. She turned and ran right into the side of that far away wooden counter, which, for some reason, was now only two or three feet away. She smashed her nose and the blow made her sit down on the floor hard. She wanted to cry, but then Trevor came up to her and put his hand on her shoulder. That hideous clown mask hung from his hand. Maybe she broke it, but right now she didn't care.

"I'm sorry. I didn't think it would scare you that bad." He sounded worried.

Laura was furious, but she let him help her to her feet. Her nose and rear end were very sore. She figured she'd have a black eye and bruises for weeks. *Maybe I won't even need a mask*, she thought.

Trevor still had the clown mask he'd scared her with. He held it out with the tips of his fingers as if it might bite him. It had two wide eyes and a bright red tongue that *only* stuck out about two inches and no more. She stared at it. *That* was what scared her? Maybe she was losing her mind. The way Trevor looked at her he probably thought the same thing.

"I don't see anybody, and nobody came, even with you yelling like that," Trevor said. "Maybe this store really is closed."

"But the door was unlocked." Laura got herself together and stood on tiptoes to look over the edge of the tall counter, the tallest counter she had ever seen in any store. She could barely see over the top. There was a doorway behind the counter, covered with a shiny black curtain. "Maybe there's a sales person back there," she said.

"Are you going back there?" Trevor's voice trembled.

"No way, Jose," she replied. "Not me. But I'll pay you a dollar if you'll go."

"I don't need a dollar," Trevor said, trying to sound tough.

She looked down into his little face, which in the dim light looked as yellow and pale as the moon. He started to walk away.

"No, don't go," she said. "You're too little to be roaming around by yourself. Even big boys would be a little scared in a place like this. Maybe we should just forget it. We can get masks at the drugstore."

"No! I want one of *these* masks!"

A breeze lifted Laura's hair. She looked around to see where the air was coming from. The shadows in the grayness appeared to be moving around, back and forth, up and down, like swaying tree limbs, or huge black birds slowly flapping their wings.

She looked back at Trevor. He screwed up his face and stuck out his lip. He'd made that ugly face at her a thousand times, probably more. His eyes were all white and bugged out, like a chicken's, although Laura had never actually seen a chicken up that close. Chicken eyes weren't like human eyes, were they? That would be weird. But Trevor's eyes were still awfully buggy. "Come on now," she said. "We're running out of time, and there's no sales clerk anywhere to help us or to take our money."

Trevor made his lip stick out even more, if that was possible. "Then we'll stay here 'til somebody shows up. We could even sleep here! Wouldn't this be a cool place to camp out?"

"Trevor, get real!"

He looked up at her with a puzzled, angry expression. "I'm *real*," he said. "Nobody made me up!"

How could anybody be so dumb? Laura thought. But she didn't say it out loud. She'd gotten into trouble before for calling her little brother stupid. And it really wasn't a nice thing to say. But when he got like this there wasn't much she could do—he was like some silly monkey. Instead she grabbed him by the hand and dragged him away from the counter and toward where she thought the door was. She glanced at her watch. It was a good watch, and she was hardly ever late for anything. "Let's just go buy our masks somewhere else, *anywhere* else," she said. "Mom and Dad will be really upset if we're late getting home."

Trevor shrieked, jerked his hand out of her grasp, and ran away. He disappeared into the hanging costumes on the other side of the store.

"Trevor! Come back here!" she cried. She was scared, much more scared than she thought she should be. She didn't run after him. She was afraid to go anywhere else in the store.

Leaving so soon? someone asked. The voice was very loud, and very close by, as if it were coming from inside her head.

Laura looked around. There was another giant clown mask hanging on a drape of blue cloth Laura hadn't noticed before. It had a pale forehead and light orange hair and shiny pink cheeks. The nose was red and swollen, as if somebody punched it over and over again. The eyes were big, black, and sad. Like an old dog's eyes.

Laura hated clowns—she'd always hated clowns. They had these big smiles painted on their faces but nobody was happy all the time so Laura knew those smiles were fake. And the so-called "funny" things they did: slapping and hitting each other, setting their big floppy shoes on fire, and dropping giant firecrackers in each other's pockets—Laura didn't think any of those things were funny at all.

The mouth in the clown mask was so big and wide it reminded her of a cave. And that was where the words were coming from, even though the mouth wasn't moving. But of course, it was a mask, and the mouths on masks didn't move, usually.

I know there must be something in my shop you'd like to buy, the clown mask said.

Laura wanted to run out of the shop as fast as she could, but she couldn't leave Trevor there. "My little brother... ran away from me. I have to... find him," she said shakily, frightened to be talking to such a creepy mask.

"They never listen, do they?" came a voice from above and to the left of the clown mask. She looked up. One of the other masks, a pale narrow one with big sleepy eyes, thin lips, and a scraggly little yellow beard growing on its pointy chin was talking to her. "But perhaps he will come back with an interesting selection." A long thin hand with bony fingers came out of the dark folds of cloth beneath the mask and made a little wave. "Welcome to Doctor Blaack's," the mask said, the pointy beard shaking, and below the mask the throat moved crazily back and forth as if there were a small animal trapped inside.

Laura stared, terrified. The way the man brayed the name Blaack—he sounded just like a goat.

He reached out to her, and she fainted to the floor.

Masks of mystery and masks of fun. Masks so silly you couldn't look at them without laughing. And masks so sad they almost made you cry. And then there were those masks so terrible, so horrible, it made you wonder how people could sell things like that, how they could stand to have those awful things in their store. Surely the people selling those masks must have had the worst nightmares of all!

Now there was Laura, looking up at one of those horrifying masks, except it wasn't a mask at all but the actual face of a human being, and she kept thinking that every time he looked into the mirror he must have made himself shudder.

"Are—are you the, the—" She couldn't think of what to say. Her brain seemed to have stopped working. "—the shopkeeper?"

"Well, a-a-actually I prefer other terms. I suppose you mi-i-ight call me a kind of *prosopologist*, one who studies the human face. Except I study the faces of all kinds of creatures, including the faces of things which are not even creatures—furniture a-a-and machines and rock faces and the like. Everything has a face, I believe, although one is not always easily recognizable. But even more specifically, my interest lies in occurrences in which someone tries on the face of another, in other words, *masks*."

Laura had no idea what he was talking about. But she thought it would be impolite to say so. She couldn't tell how tall he was because he was bowing over her, his long thin legs bent awkwardly, the way a lot of adults made themselves smaller when talking to little kids. But she wasn't a little kid—she was actually a little taller than average for her age, so she figured he must be unusually tall, taller than any adult she'd ever met in person. He was *so* skinny, and maybe a little *too* bendable. The way he moved his shoulders she thought maybe he had fewer bones than ordinary people. His head was long and narrow, and he had big teeth, just like a goat she saw once at a petting zoo.

She did what she often did when she was nervous or confused. She apologized. "I'm sorry," she said.

"Oh, he-a-avens! No need." His throat bobbed and squirmed, and Laura wondered if maybe he had a kitten trapped inside. Or a rat. Yuck!

"This place is just so crowded, but I guess you know that already."

"I prefer the term well-stocked," he said, smiling with his thin lips while his eyes looked cold and hard.

"Oh, it is," she said. "You must have everything here. But I have to go find my brother. He shouldn't be left alone."

"He'll be fine, *fine*. Where could he go? I don't have everything, I'm afraid. No one has everything—most of us learn tha-a-at, eventually. Although I ca-a-an't imagine what sort of mask I might *not* have. But certainly enough to satisfy your particular, little girl needs. Something for Halloween, or perha-a-aps something for everyday?"

She heard him call her a little girl, but she was too

scared of him to let her anger show. "Every day?" she asked. "Who would want to wear a mask every day? That's silly." Then she realized she'd been rude. "I'm s-s-sorry," she said again, stammering, thinking it probably sounded like she was making fun of his obvious speech problem.

"That's quite all ri-ight, my dear," Doctor Blaack said. "Sometimes putting on a mask permits us to forget our manners and speak whatever it is we truly feel."

"But I'm not wearing a mask," she replied.

"You were angry, but you di-i-dn't want to seem so. So you put on a mask, of sorts."

"I didn't mean to, but I guess I wanted to."

"I'm not sure intention or 'want' applies, actually. Most of us simply can't help ourselves. Most of us can't go out the door without making sure our very special mask is in place. You know what I mean, don't you little girl?"

"I'm not a little girl," she said, trying not to sound angry. "I'm a teenager," she said, although she didn't always feel like a teenager. "And no, I don't know what you mean."

Doctor Blaack chuckled, then he said, "Have you ever gone to school feeling quite sad, perhaps, or even moderately sad, but instead of frowning or looking sad you wore the biggest smile you could make?"

Laura thought about it, but only for a moment because the answer was obvious. "Well, yes. More than once I guess."

"And why did you do that, make a smile like that, when you didn't feel like smiling at all?"

"I guess I didn't want people to know I was sad."

"And why not?"

"Oh, I don't know. If they were polite, they'd ask me questions about why I looked sad, and when I'm sad I don't always want to answer a lot of questions. I want to be left alone. And if they weren't polite, if they were the kind of person who teased people when they looked sad, well, obviously I wouldn't want to give them the chance to do that to me."

"Verrry good, my dear. So your smile, it was a mask. It just wasn't a mask you put on. It was a mask you made with your face!"

"Well, when you put it that way, I guess that's true."

"Of course it is. And would it surprise you to hear that there are some people who feel they must wear a mask every hour of every day in order to hide something they are feeling, or because of some secret they don't want anyone else to know?"

Laura thought about the question for a minute. "No, that wouldn't surprise me. I think I know some people like that."

"Tha-a-at's because you're a very smart young woman. You also strike me as someone who naturally shows her feelings. Do you have a hard time hiding it when you're angry or sad? Does it seem as if the whole world knows? And when you're happy does joy burst right out of you?"

"Well, yes—I guess that's me."

"Of course! But you didn't come here to listen to an old man lecture you. You came here for a Halloween mask!"

Laura giggled. "Yes! And one for my little brother, too, if he ever shows up." She looked around nervously. What if Trevor had wandered out of the store?

"Well, certainly for a boy his age almost any costume will do." Doctor Blaack bent over quickly, his huge goatface bobbing up and down right in front of her. The move startled her so much she almost fell over. One of his big eyes winked. "Boys his age are so… indiscriminate, don't you think?"

"I, I guess."

"Hey! I'm not scrimin-whatever!" Trevor popped out from between two large, billowy costumes. They were supposed to be ghosts, maybe. It was hard to tell.

"Trevor! Where have you been? Don't wander off like that!" She glanced up at Doctor Blaack. "Sorry..."

"Quite all right, my dear. I did not mean to offend his delicate sensibilities." Doctor Blaack bowed deeply in front of Trevor. "Your pa-a-ardon, kind sir."

"You talk funny."

"Trevor!"

"Quite all right," Doctor Blaack said, although his frown said something else. So, he was putting on a mask, too, she thought. "Certainly I've had worse things said about me. I take it you are looking for a mask, young sir?"

"A special mask," Trevor replied. "You have something like that?"

"Well, I certainly like to believe that all the masks in my establishment are rather special. But let us see if I can find something particularly suitable for you. Some sort of ape or other subhuman creature perhaps?" Trevor frowned. "No? Perhaps not."

Doctor Blaack turned around and began rapidly sorting through the wall of masks and costumes, murmuring to himself as he searched for a mask for

Trevor. Laura turned her head and whispered to her brother, "Be nice." Trevor just stuck out his tongue.

"Won't do, won't do, won't do…" Doctor Blaack mumbled to himself and eventually stopped going through the hanging merchandise and slid out some dirty, battered boxes from the dark spaces underneath. Laura wondered if he was going to look at every costume in the shop just to find something to satisfy her picky little brother—which seemed like a weird way to run a business.

Doctor Blaack stared at the dusty boxes and frowned. "Now, where did I put that very special mask?"

He poked a couple of boxes with a long, terribly skinny finger, picked several up and shook them, his ear pressed against their sides. When he took his ear away it was black with dirt. *Gross!* Laura thought.

Trevor giggled. "Shhhh," Doctor Blaack said. "I'm hoping that very special mask will tell me exactly which box it is hiding in!"

"You mean it talks?" Trevor said in amazement.

"Oh, it talks, sings, even sneezes. It depends on what it needs to do at that particular moment, you see." Without another word Doctor Blaack began pulling out more boxes and running his long fingers quickly through their contents.

Laura and Trevor ran behind another row of costumes, using them as a curtain to avoid all the flying bits and pieces, pulling them back and peeking in order to watch him work. "He looks like a big crazy bird!" Trevor said, and she didn't bother to shush him because it was true. The room was soon so full of dust Laura's eyes burned and she started coughing uncontrollably, but she couldn't really see Doctor Blaack, just a flurry of movement where his arms were.

"Ah ha! I knew I'd find it!" he shouted.

The dust settled over the floor. The air began to clear. The room looked like a garbage dump, with old boxes and junky things scattered all over. And there was Doctor Blaack standing in the middle of it all, a dark shadow draped over his outstretched hands.

"You like?" he asked.

But Laura had no idea what he was holding. It didn't look like a mask at all. It appeared to breathe in and out like some big dark living thing. Like a big black bird or maybe a bat. But she couldn't tell. She couldn't see eyes or nose, ears or a mouth.

The black thing floated up out of Doctor Blaack's

hands and started flapping its way toward Trevor's face. An enormous white grin appeared in the middle of it, just like the Cheshire Cat from *Alice in Wonderland*.

Trevor yelped and ran away again, disappearing into the depths of the store. "Trevor! Come back here!" The panic in her own voice scared her even more. Soon Laura couldn't even hear his footsteps anymore. But she understood why he ran—she wouldn't want that thing touching her face either.

"Too baaad," Doctor Blaack said, sounding as if he was sad but Laura was pretty sure he was just play acting. She kind of liked Doctor Blaack—he could be funny and charming—but he could also be pretty scary, and she didn't really like it that he pretended so much. She didn't trust people who pretended all the time—you never knew how they really felt about anything.

The black thing flew back and landed on Doctor Blaack's hand. He stroked it and whispered something to it and put it back into its box. "It's actually quite gentle, and would have done anything the boy asked. I suppose your little brother isn't as indiscriminate in his choice of masks as he appears."

"I… I guess not," she replied.

Doctor Blaack stood up. He was suddenly so tall

Laura had to look practically straight up. "Of course you guess!" He smiled sadly. "Do you have any idea what *indiscriminate* means my dear?"

"I don't—not really."

"And she's as honest as the day is lo-o-o-o-o-ong!" Doctor Blaack shouted at the ceiling, his arms spread wide, palms up. He gazed down at her and smiled again. "In this case, it means he will wear almost anything, my dear, if you can convince him it is—what's the word?—*cool*."

"He won't dress up like Barbie—I tried to get him to do that year before last."

"Hmmm." Doctor Blaack scratched his pointy little beard. "But for you, my dear, who are so clever and perceptive, and mature—you have sworn this is your *last* time trick-or-treating?"

"Absolutely."

"Then for you, my dear, we must find something very special, something suitable for your retirement from this perhaps too childish activity." He pulled a tape measure from his pocket and, leaning uncomfortably close, wrapped the tape measure around her head. She was surprised and wanted to pull away from him, but she made herself stand still. He mumbled something she couldn't understand, pulled the measuring tape down the length of her face, and then rapidly measured the width of her head from her left ear to the right. He straightened up again, and much to her irritation patted her on top of her head. But before she could complain he turned his bony shoulders and moved away from her, pushing against the costumes hanging on both sides of him. They swung violently back and forth against her. She held up her arms to protect herself, sure she was about to be buried under a pile of Halloween disguises, but somehow they stayed on their hooks.

Doctor Blaack turned around. "Are you coming? You won't find the right costume here among the ordinary merchandise!"

"But what about Trevor?" Laura hurried after him, but Doctor Blaack disappeared into the swaying walls of detached faces and weird bodies. She was afraid of getting lost, so she rushed forward a little faster than she should have, stumbled, and fell, sliding a couple of feet along the floor under all those hanging costumes.

With a struggle she managed to turn herself over and found herself in complete darkness. She was terrified. She turned her head left and right and couldn't find a glow or a glimmer or even a ghost of a light.

Then a form came rushing out of the darkness, all knees and elbows as it did its string puppet moves. As the figure drew closer, it became clear that this was Doctor Blaack. He held something in his hands.

"So what will Laura wear for her very la-ast Halloween?" he sang. "Perhaps something musical?" He thrust a mask in front of her. It was a girl's head—her huge mouth making a silly grin, and stuck into her mouth there were seven or eight horns playing a variety of tunes. She even had a small horn jammed into each ear, and these were playing loudly, and harshly, more noise than music. And just to make the whole thing even more ridiculous two mechanical birds on loops of wire were flying around her head singing along.

"Or perhaps something chronometrical?" Doctor Blaack shouted. The musical mask disappeared, and in its place there was a girl's head that had been turned into a cuckoo clock. Her hair looked like roof shingles and there were numbers painted on her face. Clock hands turned from a black post sticking out of the tip of her nose and her eyes crossed when the hands passed over them. Every few seconds her mouth flew open and her tongue came out, stiff as a diving board, with this goofy looking bird perched at the end. The bird would look at the oversized wristwatch strapped to its wing, and go "Coo Coo!" so loudly it made its beak wrinkle. Then it winked and the tongue slid back and the mouth shut, and the mask's eyes closed. Then the show started all over again.

With Laura as a captive audience (Where could she go? It was so dark she couldn't even see her feet!) Doctor Blaack demonstrated mask after mask in quick succession: a "magical" mask with a bunny hopping out of the top of the hat-shaped head, an "insect" mask made up of hundreds of flapping butterflies, an "agricultural" mask consisting of flowering plants, corn cobs, and cabbage with singing bees, and an "eggs-it-stenshul" mask whose weeping egg faces made so much sad noise she wanted to smash and scramble them to shut them up. Each was more complicated, and far stranger than the last.

"Could I . . . could I just get something a little simpler?" she asked. "More dignified?"

"Oh." The masks all disappeared. Doctor Blaack stood before her scratching his head. "Why didn't . . ."

". . . you say so?" And they were back in the store again, standing in an aisle between costumes, maybe in the same spot they were before—she couldn't tell.

She was so confused. She didn't know how to answer him. "I don't know. Too many choices?"

"Hmmm. Choices are a good thing, my dear, but sometimes they do require a lot of work in order to make them. But I'm sure we'll have just the thing, given your age, hmmm...and your insistence that you are no longer a child." He reached up and began pulling things off a shelf she hadn't even realized was there. Several boxes dropped into his outstretched hands. He shuffled through them rapidly, tossing some of them up into the shadows, where they must have found a shelf to land on since they didn't come back down. He was left with a single clear plastic box, which he handed to her.

It took a moment for her eyes to adjust so that she could see through the plastic into the dark insides of the box. She almost dropped it when a too-real, too-familiar face peered up at her, like the drowned face of a beautiful young woman under the surface of a sparkling pool.

"Mom?" She felt her eyes fill with tears. The face looked like her mother's face when her mother was younger. Laura loved going through the photo albums at home and looking at pictures of her mom and dad when they were just kids, and later in high school and college. Her mom had had such a gentle, lovely face, identical to the one in the box she was now holding.

"It's my mother! How did you get a mask with my mother's face on it?"

"No, my child. No—look more closely. There are differences."

Laura held the box closer and squinted. There were some differences—the nose was a little fuller, the ears pushed out a little more from the face, the eyes—"It's like me," she said. "But not exactly. It's older—"

"Exa-actly," he said. "Perhaps this will be you when you're a few years older. Perhaps not, who knows? Who can predict the future?"

It was a little scary but also wonderful. "But how could you have a mask like this in your shop?"

"Trade secret. But the mask is alive. It has intelligence, of a sort. It likes to mirror people, if you will. While you were looking at it, trying to find it down in its shadowy home, it was adapting to you. Had anyone else been holding the box, that mask would look very different now. But are you pleased? That's what's important. And I must make my living—shall I ring it up for you?"

"Of course, yes, well—how much is it?"

"Oh, I'm sure you will have enough. Step to the back, please, to the cash register."

Laura followed Doctor Blaack through more rows of hanging costumes, under several arches made up of fake arms and legs and tentacles and long, flowing wigs, to the big counter again. The cash register looked even larger than it had before—it was as big as the huge TV they had in the living room at home. And a beautiful old gold color with keys as big as quarters. Every time Doctor Blaack pushed one of these enormous clattering keys a metal sign the size of a playing card and shaped like a tombstone popped up inside a long glass box attached to the top of the cash register. Each of these signs had a large number printed on it, except one that displayed a decimal point. "Ten dollars, it seems," Doctor Blaack said thoughtfully. "Do you have that much, young lady?"

That was the exact amount she'd put aside for her own costume. She eagerly reached into her jeans pocket for the money as Doctor Blaack hit another, even larger key with his fist.

A bell mounted on the wall clanged loudly as the cash drawer rolled open slowly, sounding like a train car rumbling down the tracks. "Wait!" she cried.

Doctor Blaack peered down at her, frowning. "All sales are final."

"Oh, I still want it. I have enough money." She pulled out a twenty dollar bill. "But I have to pay for Trevor's too!"

"Yesssss, but where is he?"

Laura looked around. There was still no sign of her little brother. It had been a while since he'd run off—she couldn't believe she'd forgotten that. She should have kept looking for him. "He was scared by your, well, that thing you had."

Doctor Blaack lowered his huge face to her level. "Waass? But what about isss?"

"Trevor? Where are you? It's time to go!" she yelled. She looked up at Doctor Blaack. "Sorry—just let me round him up." Laura moved quickly back under the arches and into the aisles of costumes.

Sometimes fear made you ridiculous. Sometimes fear made you imagine the worst, strangest, most impossible things: your house on fire, your family in danger, faces that looked like masks and masks that looked like faces, your brother vanished, fallen through a dark hole in the world. It was all her fault for not going after him.

"Trevor!" She'd been calling him for what seemed

like ten minutes or more. She was responsible for her little brother and she had to find him.

She went down the aisle where she thought she'd last seen him. This section of the store appeared to be devoted to science-fiction costumes—there were robot costumes and all kinds of aliens—big brain heads and heads like insects, four-armed and six-armed, tentacles and claws and hands that looked like guns—and costumes based on every science fiction TV show or movie she'd ever seen or heard of. Her dad had always liked stuff like that—he said that sometimes we treat other people like they're from an alien planet, as if there's no way we can ever understand how they think about things, and how sad and unfortunate that was.

Trevor loved this kind of stuff too so she got her hopes up. Surely he'd want to check these out. She went up and down the aisles, shouting his name, pulling costumes apart and moving boxes around in case he was hiding, but Trevor was nowhere to be seen.

The next aisle over was movie monster costumes—Dracula and Frankenstein and guys like that. Trevor loved that kind of stuff even more, but still there was no sign of him anywhere. "Trevor! Where are you?" she shouted, but hearing her own voice all scared like that made her want to start crying, so she stopped.

"Miss! Back here!" Doctor Blaack's face suddenly appeared at the distant end of the aisle, his clothes so black they made his body disappear so it was like his bodiless head was floating in the air. "I think he's back in the storage room!"

Laura hurried down the aisle, following Doctor Blaack through a gray, haze-filled doorway in the back wall she hadn't noticed before. "I don't normally permit customers in here. It's private," he said sternly. "But apparently your little brother has a way of finding himself where he most assuredly does not belong."

Should she be following this tall, scary man into a dark room like this? *Stranger danger, Laura!* she thought. But she had to find Trevor. Looking around the gigantic, cave-like room with all its dust and hanging cobwebs, Laura wondered why anyone would want to come back here in the first place. Doctor Blaack's back room was a bigger mess even than his store. Boxes were piled everywhere. Broken pieces of masks and costumes crunched under her feet. Large sheets covered a lot of the stuff on the floor, as well as several tables. At first Laura thought the sheets were black, but it was only because there was so much greasy dust caked on them. Grimy boxes were stacked everywhere. The windows had been boarded up, and the only light came from a bare light bulb overhead that had been painted red. The red light made everything look hot, as if the room were ready to burst into flames any second. And it was all so dim she could barely see the floor under her ghostly white tennis shoes. There were even more masks and costumes hanging from the ceiling and lined up against the walls like prisoners of war.

Maybe it was just all the dust (so thick on the shoulders of some of the costumes it looked like gray snow, or the world's worst case of dandruff) and the lack of light, but it seemed to her that these costumes were a lot older than the ones Doctor Blaack displayed out on the main floor. These masks were decorated with fancy drawings and complicated patterns and faded, antique-looking colors, and the clothing that went with the masks was definitely old-timey. And some of the costumes appeared to have mechanical parts—hinged metal strips and clockwork pieces with rusty surfaces— that made them look quite old indeed.

"He's over there," Doctor Blaack was suddenly beside her, his arm stretched out straight and looking impossibly long, like a pole with some wiggling fingers at the end. One of the fingers pointed at a small, hunched-over figure near the wall. "Beakman discovered him."

"Beakman?"

"My…um…assistant. He stays back here, usually doesn't deal directly with customers."

Laura hadn't seen anyone else in the store—she'd just assumed Doctor Blaack ran it by himself. But she couldn't worry over that right now. Trevor was standing by himself, hunched over with his face in his hands. It looked like he was crying, the way his back was shaking, but he wasn't making a sound. She ran over to him, pushing past a mannequin in the middle of the floor wearing a scary-looking costume and mask—all beak and feathers and those giant eyes!—and stood next to him, putting an arm over his shoulders. "What's wrong, honey? What happened?"

He really had her scared. She'd never called him honey before.

Trevor turned his head around. He was wearing this face mask—a cartoon mouse character. It wasn't Mickey—it was more rat-like than Mickey, with its long pointy snout and its scared red eyes. But no, those weren't the mouse's eyes—those were Trevor's eyes looking out through the mask's eye holes. They were wet and red because Trevor had been crying. But more than that, Trevor's eyes looked trapped inside the mask. He was terrified.

"I—can't—get it off!" he cried in kind of a high-pitched, squeaky voice that echoed inside the pointy end.

"Oh dear," Doctor Blaack said behind her. "I really wish he haaadn't put thaaat one on."

In a dark, dark wood there was a dark, dark house; And in the dark, dark house there was a dark, dark room;

And in the dark, dark room there was a dark, dark cupboard;

And in the dark, dark cupboard there was a dark, dark shelf;

And on the dark, dark shelf there was a dark, dark box; And in the dark, dark box there was a...mouse!

Sometimes it seemed the world was just too full of eyes. Looking at you or not looking at you, watching everything you did each and every day or maybe just ignoring you completely. The eyes of parents, loving you but still you sometimes wished they didn't look at you so much. The eyes of strangers, and you wondered what those strangers might be thinking. Eyes that glowed in the dark, watching you from the woods when you passed there late at night. And the eyes of people that you really wanted to notice you, but it seemed like they almost never did.

And sometimes eyes looked at you at the absolute worst times—when your hair was a mess, or you'd just done something stupid, or when you'd been crying, and you didn't want anybody to be looking at you at all.

The way Trevor was looking at her now, it was like all those things together. He looked so embarrassed over what he had done, and so scared. And so needing her to help him, but Laura had no idea what to do.

"I put it on—it was just lying there. I put it on and *now* I can't get it *off*! Laura, get it off me! *Please?*" He put his little hands up to the sides of the mask and pushed and pushed, his fingers getting red and sweaty and slipping off. But the mask was stuck tight, like it was glued to his skin. Maybe it actually was glued to his skin! His small eyes—had they always been this small?—moved around inside the mask's big eyeholes, as if they were trying to find some way to escape.

"Doctor Blaack?" Laura cried. "Could you do something? He can't get it off!" She felt like a helpless little girl. She hated that.

"Beakman!" Doctor Blaack yelled. "Beakman, get over here! How did you let this happen?"

And that was when that really scary costume she'd passed— the one that had been all beak and feathers and giant eyes, like a big crow, she guessed, or a magpie— hustled over with a loud squawk and a big flapping sound and pushed her out of the way. She thought she might scream. She wanted to scream but kept it in. The way this monster bent over Trevor with its giant head and its long pointy yellow beak—sharp as a knife blade!— and its eyes like big black saucers floating in a bowl of bright yellow soup, it looked like it was going to peck her little brother and gobble him up like he was just a wiggly bug or something!

"Beakman! Take care of him!" Doctor Blaack yelled, and that made Laura panic even more. Was Doctor Blaack ordering this monster to hurt Trevor?

The monster bird planted a giant foot with three big clawed toes on either side of Trevor, straddling him. Then he lowered his big black wings and hands appeared. He grabbed each side of the mask attached to Trevor's face and yanked. Trevor started crying.

"Doctor, it won't budge!" the monster bird cried with the voice of a squeaky little man. Laura knew she would have laughed out loud if she hadn't been so scared, and that would've been awful.

"Try harder!" Doctor Blaack commanded, and when the monster bird still struggled he joined in helping, grabbing the mask and tugging on it as well. Still, with no progress being made, Laura pushed in between them and she grabbed it too, at least as well as she could, with one hand around the mouse mask nose and another on one corner of its ridiculous smiling mouth. It felt weird—soft as fur but stiff as hard plastic at the same time. It seemed to her particularly bizarre that the mouse mask would smile so much with all this going on.

"It's okay, Trevor. We'll get it off, I promise!" she said, but she wasn't sure of that. She just wanted to make Trevor stop crying.

They pulled and they yanked and it was a particularly bad experience because the giant bird smelled of dust and mold and its ragged feathers kept getting into Laura's ears, nose, and mouth, and Doctor Blaack smelled a little too, like old cheese maybe, or maybe it was goat, not that Laura had ever gotten close enough to a goat to smell one before.

Suddenly the mouse mask started laughing. And it was strange because she could tell Trevor wasn't laughing—it was the mask all by itself. It laughed so hard it was howling, and just generally wiggling around so much that first Beakman's hands slipped off and the bird went flying backwards, and then Doctor Blaack lost his balance and tumbled away, and then Laura, as hard as she held on with all her strength as the mouse mask laughed and roared and finally started sneezing—*gross gross gross!*—her hands slipped off too and she fell flat on her backside.

And just like that the mouse mask was calm again, still and motionless like any regular old mask, with her little brother Trevor still trapped inside. But wasn't the mask larger than before? It sure was—it had grown to cover his ears and part of his hair.

"What—what kind of mask is that?" she asked, annoyed at the quake she heard in her voice.

"Well my dear," Doctor Blaack said in almost a whisper (And why was he whispering? Was he afraid the mask might hear?), "Obviously it's the kind of mask a curious little boy shouldn't put on."

And that was just a little too much. Laura couldn't help it—she started to cry too. Just a little. "What'll we do?"

"There, there." Doctor Blaack put one of those long, bony hands on her shoulder. It made her nervous, but she let the hand stay there. "I must apologize. I like things to run smoothly, and when they do not I sometimes forget my manners. It's just that my assistant, Mr. *Beakman*, has a rather simple job, which is to watch the stock in the backroom and to prevent just this sort of thing from happening. Now, that doesn't sound too difficult, does it? Of course not. Hardly anyone ever comes back here. Why, no one's been back here in years."

"Years, but your shop hasn't been open—" Laura began.

"It's a bit too complicated to explain during a crisis, my dear. But in any case, I assure you, such a mishap has not occurred in many years. But our Mr. Beakman knows the cautions which must be taken. And surely, he of all people should know what might happen if a young lad were to try on something that must not be tried on, ever! I put the blame on him, not young Trevor."

Laura twisted around to stare at Beakman. He was leaning forward, his giant beak hanging down like it was far too heavy for his head to lift. That's when she was sure this wasn't some monstrous bird, but just a little man with a costume on. She could see the scrawny shoulders rising above where the wings were attached, and the knobby knees showing through the dark tights, and the shaky hands coming out of the ends of the wings, and if she tilted her head just right she could spy a little past those big black saucer pupils where the man's eyes were hiding, trapped and scared just like Trevor's.

So had Beakman done the same thing Trevor had? Had he walked in here years ago, a little boy who'd put on the wrong costume and never been able to get out of it? And so now he had to work here forever?

Laura really needed to know but she was too afraid to ask. "But what do we do?"

"Well—" Doctor Blaack was up now, pacing. "In your brother's particular case, I'd suggest nothing."

"Nothing? You're not going to help him?"

"Oh, I didn't say that. Although the bad news is we can't remove the mask, the good news is it will fall off by itself at the end of Halloween night. Midnight, to be precise. He's lucky in that the consequences—erm, effects—of these things are generally time limited. We'll just keep him here in the shop, feeding him adequately I assure you, provide him with regular bathroom breaks, whatever his physical needs might be. Perhaps we could add him to the window display, as a more animated element? Has your brother ever shown an interest in acting?"

"Well, he was a sheep in the church play," Laura said doubtfully.

"A sheep? Splendid!"

"No, no, it's not splendid at all! He can't just stay here!"

"Oh, but we'll take very good care of him. Especially if he's part of the window display."

"No. No! He has to come home with me! Halloween's not until tomorrow night. I'll be in *so much* trouble if I leave him here."

Doctor Blaack stared at her, one bony hand absently pulling on his chin as if he were trying to make it even longer. "I fail to see the difficulty," he declared.

"He's *seven*. I'm barely a *teenager*. We live with our *parents*."

"And you believe that these—these *parents*—might

feel something were amiss if he doesn't return home with you?"

"Of course they would! Trevor's just a little kid!" She didn't want to raise her voice to this scary-looking goat-man, but *come on.*

"Well, then. I suppose that would be a problem." He paced some more, then stopped, raising one long forefinger into the air as if he were testing the direction of the wind. "Then I suppose I could rent you the mask until it comes off."

"Rent? You're kidding. I can't—"

Beakman pushed past her and appeared to be whispering something into Doctor Blaack's ear. He was forced to turn his head sideways to keep his long bill out of the way. Then Beakman stepped away and quickly disappeared into the shadows.

Doctor Blaack straightened up and looked at her sternly. An enormous grin spread across his face, splitting the dried-out skin. "Did I say rent? Oh heavens no—I meant lend. I will *lend* Trevor this mask until the entire matter is settled, one way, or the other."

Have you seen the ghost of John?
Long white bones and the rest all gone,
Ooh, ooh, wouldn't it be chilly with no skin on?

Expectation can make you giddy. Expectation can be nothing more than a dream. When whatever you wished for finally happens it's never as good as what you expected, or as long-lasting, but it was still fun anticipating it, wasn't it? Like every great cook knows, anticipation can be the most delicious part of any good meal.

But when what you're expecting is something terrible, like having to tell your parents that your younger brother—the one you were in charge of—now has a mask stuck on his face that no one seems able to remove no matter what, expectation is just the absolute worst.

On their way to the bus stop Laura tried her best to calm Trevor down, but she was having a hard time just keeping herself calm. She was so nervous she kept dropping the box with that pretty mask she'd bought for herself. Every time she looked at Trevor the mouse mask covered a little more of his head. It spread behind his ears and down his neck and about half of his head was covered, leaving only the back of his head exposed. Soon her little brother would be wearing an entire mouse head!

"We'll just tell Mom and Dad what happened," Laura said. "We'll tell them I lost track of you for just a minute, and you tried on a mask in the store where we told them we were, in fact, going with their permission—we weren't doing anything wrong—and for some reason we don't understand it just got stuck. And the two adults in the store—I guess that Beakman fellow is an adult, under that ugly bird costume—they couldn't get it off either. So what could we do? We came right home, just like we knew they'd want us to do. I'll tell them I should have watched you better. I'll tell them it was my fault."

"Th—thanks," Trevor said beside her, his voice echoing inside the mouse mask. "But what if—if they can't get it—get it off, either?"

"Oh, I wouldn't worry about that. Mom and Dad have had experience with practically everything—why I bet Dad must have gotten a mask stuck on his face a time or two when he was a little boy. He's always talking about how he used to get into things when he was a kid, and getting into trouble. And they're both good with tools."

"Tools!" Trevor's voice sounded full of terror.

"Sorry, sorry. I didn't mean tools, really. I should have said—um—lubricants, lotions, oil and grease, things like that. That's what they use to make things slippery. I'll bet if they use the right kind that dumb mask'll just slide right off you."

"But what if—if it doesn't?"

"Then they'll take you to the fire department—the fire department helps kids stuck inside things all the time. Or maybe they'll just take you to the hospital. The doctors there, they know about all kinds of emergencies."

"Is this a 'mergency?"

"Kind of. But not the real serious kind. I mean, you're not really hurt or anything. You just want that thing off your face right away." Laura felt really bad for him. Usually Trevor was just completely obnoxious. But right now he seemed pitiful. They were only a couple of blocks from the bus stop. "We'd better hurry now," she said. "If we're late they'll be worried."

But they hadn't gone more than a few steps when something fuzzy and floppy ran out of the side street in front of them, tripped, and sprawled face-first across the sidewalk. It was a terrible fall, and whoever, or whatever, it was, wasn't getting up quickly.

Trevor pulled on Laura's arm and pointed. "It's that big bird from the store."

Laura looked more closely. Trevor was right. "Beak— Mr. Beakman? Are you okay?" The bird costume just groaned softly. Laura hurried over with Trevor following slightly behind. She put one arm under a bent wing and struggled to get Mr. Beakman off the sidewalk. Trevor ran to the other side and helped by pushing up beneath the other wing.

"Careful, Trevor. He might have broken something."

"I'm glad—I'm so glad—I caught you," Mr. Beakman said breathlessly. "Before—it was too late." His voice was weak and a little raspy, but it was clearly an adult voice, although Laura had no idea how old. It was a little hard to listen to, coming from somewhere so deep inside the big mask, and there was just this little hole at the end of the long beak where the sound came out. *How does this poor man eat?* She wondered.

"Too late for what, Mr. Beakman?" she asked.

"For what, for what I'm supposed to tell you," he replied.

"Mr. Beakman, could you hurry?" Laura asked. "Sorry, but we can't miss our bus."

"It's just that—" Mr. Beakman started wheezing, and with each wheeze a spray of small, wilted feathers shot out of the end of his beak.

"Laura! We'll be late!" Trevor tugged on her hand.

"Doctor Blaack—sent me. He forgot—important." The tiny feathers were coming out rapidly now, swirling around between the three of them like a cloud of fuzzy snow. Laura heard Mr. Beakman take a deep, painful-sounding breath, then he spoke rapidly during the exhale. "You can't tell anyone. Leave it alone and it'll drop off—midnight, Halloween. Annoy it—it's stubborn—anger it and it might never let go of his face!"

"How so?"

"It's magic."

"Mr. Beakman!" Laura gasped. "That's kind of important information!"

"I know—" He shook his head, the big beak wobbling unsteadily. "He's sorry—he forgets things sometimes, and the rules—they can be so complicated. But this— never happens—at least not since—" He stopped then.

"Since *you*, Mr. Beakman?" she asked. But instead of answering, he waddled off, still wheezing, taking his cloud of ragged tiny feathers with him. But just as she was turning around he yelled back, "Good luck!"

The bus was about half full and they sat in the back, away from everybody else on the way home so that they could talk. Laura noticed how the other passengers looked curiously at Trevor when he climbed on board wearing his mask, but then smiled as he walked past. "How cute!" one old lady said to her friend in a not very quiet whisper. Trevor appeared to tense up when she said that, but kept on moving, his head nodding forward from the weight of the long snout.

Laura checked her watch. She could do this. She could make this happen. "We have to come up with a reason why you're wearing that mask early, and all the time," she said as soon as they sat down.

"Don't you remember? I'm wearing it cause I can't take it off!" he said in a strained whisper.

"I know that, Trevor! But we can't tell people that, especially not Mom and Dad! You heard Mr. Beakman." She stared at him. Now the mask covered almost a third of the back of his head, and his whiskers were longer, fuller. This whole situation was so frustrating. He was being a little dense, but it was because he was so scared— she knew what that was like.

"Maybe we could tell them we saw a mouse in the house and it freaked you out so now I'm disguising myself as a giant, mean-looking mouse so I can scare all those little ones away."

Oh, please, she thought, but what she said was, "Well, that's a very original idea, Trevor. But maybe that's a little too original for Mom and Dad. I mean, they're not like parents in the movies—they work in offices."

"It might freak them out too much, huh?"

"Exactly. But they like to think of themselves as flexible, and a little out of the ordinary. They'll do something out of the ordinary if there's a good cause behind it."

"Like dolphins and world peace," Trevor said.

"Exactly. Or if they think it's for our benefit, you

and me. Remember when you were really sick and you wanted to go to the circus but you couldn't?"

"No, I was too little. But I've seen those pictures of Dad."

"Right! Dressed up like a clown. Because you couldn't go to the circus he brought a little bit of the circus home to you. He wore that silly thing all day—he even sat down to dinner in it. I remember that he ended up getting white and red clown makeup smeared all over his chicken drumstick at dinner, but he still ate it!"

They both laughed, which got them a few curious glances from the other passengers. Laura started whispering again. "So, what if you told them you wanted to wear the mask to school tomorrow? I mean, it *really is* 'Wear Your Costume to School Day' tomorrow."

"But I wasn't going to. It was going to be too embarrassing."

"I know, I know—I wasn't going to either. I think the custom is a little goofy, frankly. But if it'll help, I'll wear mine too, okay? But see, this is perfect! They know you're too shy, but you're going to tell them you want to try wearing it as much as possible, tonight, so that maybe by tomorrow you'll feel brave enough to wear it to school! They'll think that's a very creative solution to your problem. They'll totally go for it!"

"I don't know," he said, looking down—at least he must have been looking down because the long mouse snout was pointing at the floor of the bus. "That sounds a lot like lying, and you're always saying you should never trust a liar."

Laura knew that Trevor would be so worried about being trapped in the mask, lying wouldn't feel like such a big deal, but she didn't want to tell him that. "Well, yes, it is lying. But it's for a good cause. I know you don't want to wear that thing forever."

"Nooo. Sure. But I'm not sure I can say all that—I'd be too nervous."

"It's a long bus ride. Practice it in your head. It's like wearing that mask. You have to do it a long time before you feel comfortable."

"Mr. Beakman—he doesn't look comfortable," Trevor said, and that was practically all they said for the rest of the bus ride. By the time they reached the bus stop near their house Laura saw that the mask now enclosed her little brother's head completely. It was an actual *mouse head* now.

Mom was just getting dinner on the table when they

walked in the front door. Dad was just coming down the stairs, saw them, and collapsed with obviously faked surprise and shock. "Wow, Trevor! That's one scary mouse! It must be terrifying even to wear it!"

Laura winced. *Dad, if you only knew.*

"And Laura! Why I think your mask may even be scarier!"

"Very funny, Dad. Mine is in the box."

Her dad got up and stood close to her, pretending to examine her face. "Are you sure?" He reached over and gently grabbed a little bit of her cheek and tugged. "Well it certainly seems to be firmly attached. Trevor, is yours this well attached?" Their dad reached for Trevor's mask but Laura grabbed his arm. "Careful, Dad. That one's delicate. Don't want to mess it up."

Dad grinned. "You're right. Want everything perfect for the big night. But it's almost dinner. Trevor, go put your mask someplace safe and then join us at the table."

Trevor just stared at their dad, shuffling his feet back and forth.

"Trevor? Is something wrong?"

Laura grabbed her father's arm and tugged. "Dad, could I talk to you in private for a second?"

They went around the corner into the living room.

Trevor was listening in—she could see the tip of the mouse snout pushing its way over the edge of the doorway as if it were tracking them by smell.

Dad looked worried, which was rare for him, but she'd never pulled him aside like this before. She guessed nobody was going to act normal tonight, but it wasn't a normal night. The look on his face made her feel so guilty she almost didn't go through with it, but how could she tell him the crazy truth?

"Trevor wasn't going to wear his mask tomorrow for costume day—he said he'd be way too embarrassed. But I tried to convince him this would be good for him—face his fears, you know? And we figured out that just maybe, maybe, if he got used to wearing the mask around the house tonight, you know, doing normal stuff, he might feel a lot more comfortable about wearing it tomorrow." She made herself smile eagerly.

Much to her relief her dad smiled back. "I get it. It's the way an actor sometimes prepares for a part. Complete immersion into the character. Very creative, honey." And then he made an exaggerated wink and tried to make his smile all sly and mysterious. It looked ridiculous—an actor he was not.

"Um—yeah, thanks. I thought so." She nodded a

little too enthusiastically. She guessed she wasn't much of an actor herself.

"Great! I'll run around to the kitchen and clue your mother in so that she knows to act normally. You're a good sister, you know?"

Embarrassed, she replied, "I'm trying, Dad. I'm trying."

He walked quickly the other way toward the kitchen while she ran back to the entry hall and gave Trevor the OK sign. "He's okay with it," she whispered. "He's going around to tell Mom. Just act like everything's okay, okay? Act like the whole thing's fun."

He nodded weakly, not looking like he was having fun at all. She sighed. It wasn't likely to get better so it would have to do. Dad came around the corner. "Well!" He exhaled loudly. "I see we're all dressed for dinner!" Laura tried not to roll her eyes. "Shall we?" He bowed slightly and waved them toward the dining room.

Their mom went along with it well enough, but Laura could tell she was a little suspicious about the whole thing. She watched Trevor as he tried to eat his dinner, then she'd glance at Laura, her lips kind of twitchy as if she wanted to ask "what's going on here?"

Trevor was having problems trying to eat through

the mask. When they first started dinner, and their mom passed around the bowls of minestrone soup, Laura began to feel a little panicky. She'd been thinking about Mr. Beakman, and that little hole at the end of his mask, and wondering about how the poor man could possibly eat, and it suddenly struck her—what if Trevor couldn't eat? There was a mouth in the mask, alright, but there was darkness inside the opening, and you couldn't see Trevor's own mouth through that opening. Obviously there was air passing through, however—Trevor could still breathe, and she had no trouble hearing his voice. It didn't sound muffled at all. But that didn't necessarily mean he could eat through that mouse head. Was her little brother going to starve?

And it didn't exactly reassure her that Trevor just stared at the bowl of soup when it was placed in front of him, like he had no idea what it was. He didn't even pick up the spoon, as if he really was a mouse who had never had to use a spoon before.

Their dad looked vaguely amused, as if he understood that this was a problem Trevor was going to have to figure out. Of course he had no idea how serious a problem it might be.

Finally, Trevor grabbed a spoon, dipped it into the

soup and brought it into his mouth—or at least the mouth of the mask. When he took the spoon away it was empty. Laura waited in anticipation. After a few seconds she saw soup oozing out of the bottom of the mask where there was a small gap under Trevor's chin.

Trevor grabbed his napkin and quickly wiped the soup off his skin, without saying anything that might draw attention to his problem. But of course everybody was watching him and very much aware of his immediate problem.

Not giving up, Trevor dipped his spoon into the soup again and brought it to the mouth of the mask. *Good for you, Trev,* Laura thought. But this time he brought his other hand up and pulled the mask back a little more against his face. Obviously then, there was some space to move around in in there. Suddenly the pink profile of Trevor's lips appeared out of the darkness inside the mask and touched the front edge of the spoon. He tipped the spoon and Laura saw the swallow move down Trevor's neck. So at least he was going to be able to eat soup. She looked over at her dad, who was smiling like a goof—obviously he had been watching Trevor closely too, and now that Trevor had conquered eating soup, their dad appeared satisfied enough to focus on his own food.

But of course he didn't know what was really going on. Laura couldn't relax until she knew for sure her little brother was going to be okay, and that wouldn't be until midnight tomorrow, when Halloween was over. She never would have thought she'd be anxious for the holiday to end. How strange it was that a trip into a shop full of masks would have changed all that.

The main course was spaghetti, Trevor's favorite, but she wasn't surprised to see him take a smaller helping this time. She watched anxiously as he tried to get it into his mouth, and thought it was pretty funny the way his little tongue kept trying to grab it, kind of like an elephant's trunk, but once he got one end into his mouth he eagerly sucked in the rest. Then at the end, when he had a couple of strands of spaghetti that had gotten loose and stuck to the outside of the mask, and when she was just wondering if Trevor was going to have to use his free hand to scrape them off (but she hoped he wouldn't try to eat them after that), the mask trembled a little bit, just a little so she didn't think anyone else noticed, and the lower half of the mask just below that big long nose kind of squirmed, which made those spaghetti strands loose enough they just slid right into the mouth.

Laura stared. This wasn't a rubber mask—when they tried to pry it off her little brother's face it had been firm and hard. No way could it move like this!

Trevor grabbed a bread stick and that caused an even more dramatic reaction from the mask. When the bread stick was about a half-inch away from the mask the giant mouse lips stretched forward like a kiss and grabbed the bread, pulling it down rapidly inside the greedy mouse mouth. At least the mask chewed it a little—there was no way Trevor could have swallowed something that big that fast without choking. That mask just loved bread sticks! Was the mouse coming alive? And if it did, what would happen to Trevor?

Laura stood up hurriedly. "Sorry to eat and run, but we're planning some things together tomorrow. We have to plan, and we'll be going to bed early."

Dad started, "I think it's just great when a brother and a sister..." but Laura didn't hear the rest. She had already grabbed Trevor's hand and pulled him toward the stairs.

Once she got Trevor safely inside her room she turned him around, knelt down, and tried to find his eyes inside the eye holes of the mouse head. "Trevor, are you okay?"

"Kind of," he said wearily. "I didn't get that much to eat—just a little soup. I don't know where most of it went—I think the mask ate it."

"Sorry. I'll sneak you up a milkshake later with a really long straw. That way we can make sure your lips are on the straw and that this thing doesn't get any."

The mask made a thunderous burp.

"That wasn't me," Trevor said.

"I figured it wasn't," she said.

"What if I starve?" Trevor asked sadly. Laura looked down through the mask's large eyeholes into the deep shadows where Trevor's smaller eyes blinked sleepily, lost and scared. It about broke her heart.

"You won't. I won't let you. You're still pretty hungry, huh?" Trevor nodded vigorously. "Wait, I think I've got a brownie." She went over to her dresser and opened the top drawer, pulled out a brownie wrapped in clear plastic and brought it back. "I got some at the store a couple of days ago. These are probably terrible for you, bad for me, too. Mom would freak. But I had the munchies, you know?" Trevor nodded vigorously again. "I'm probably

contributing to the delinquency of a minor or something, but this is an emergency right?"

Trevor shook the bed he nodded so hard.

"Definitely," she said and unwrapped the brownie.
But when she brought it up to his face the mask came
alive again. The mouse's nose wrinkled up several times,
kind of like an accordion, then the mouth stretched out
toward the brownie until Laura pulled it away.

"It wants my brownie!" Trevor said from inside
the mask.

"Well, it can't have it," she said. She went over to her
dresser and grabbed a wooden hairbrush. "I'm going
to try something." With the brownie in one hand and
the brush in the other, the handle sticking forward, she
brought them both toward the mouse mask. When the
mouth of the mask opened up to grab the brownie she
jammed the handle of the brush into the side of the
mouth. The mask struggled a little, but couldn't bite
down any further. Trevor's lips appeared on the other
side of the opening and Laura proceeded to feed him a
little bit of brownie at a time.

"So it may be a magical mask," she said, laughing,
feeling clever, "but it's still not smarter than me."

*M*ore orange than she'd ever seen in one place, in maybe her entire life. Black old-timey letters on the orange canvas banner that covered the brick front of the school: "*HALLOWEEN IN AMERICA*", bats and cats and crows and black witch silhouettes around the border. But that was just a taste, a tease to prepare her appetite for orange. Just inside the door began a flash flood of orange: pumpkin orange and carrot orange and yam orange, marigold orange, goldfish orange, and monarch butterfly orange. Cheese orange and fire orange and zinnia orange and even Irish setter orange. And the roundest, plumpest, juiciest orangey oranges, dripping sweet and delicious citrus paradise goodness!

The All Hallows decoration committee had really outdone themselves this season. Every year this group of teachers and older students chose a theme for Halloween. They worked on displays for months, hiding them in storage rooms and under tarps until the day before Halloween. They worked for hours putting it all together to present to the rest of the school the following morning.

This year's theme was "Halloween in America" and it was about how America had taken the holiday over from the countries and traditions where it all began and transformed it into something very American. Partly that meant it became more commercial in America—people figured out how to make money out of it, but she guessed there were other changes too.

The committee had borrowed historic pieces from private collectors and library collections and the antique stores in town and made some special exhibits of their own to create this "Halloween Experience" (anyway that's what Principal Figg called it). There were old costumes and antique rubber masks hanging on the walls, and big advertising pieces and all kinds of posters and greeting cards and Halloween decorations from past decades. Of course they had to be very careful with these things, so to protect them there were "guards" posted around the school in ghost costumes with badges, older kids mostly, some who took their "guarding" a little too seriously in her opinion. But most of the students behaved pretty well—after all, almost nobody wanted it canceled except maybe a few people in town. Halloween was too much fun!

As soon as she entered the door with Trevor she saw tons of pumpkins cut out of bright orange construction paper hanging on strings from the ceiling, with real pumpkins carved with hideous faces on small side tables by the lockers. There were even a couple of carved turnips like the old Irish used before they came over and discovered that the pumpkins in America worked better for carving. Down the hall, wall decorations devoted to the Mexican *Day of the Dead* with skeletons and skulls crowded the walls, and further on cutout silhouettes of witches and plague rats, haunted houses with red window eyes, a pumpkin head on a dancing skeleton body, and a giant antique advertising poster showing a red devil smoking a cigarette (which Principal Figg later ordered taken down).

A table covered with orange cloth, decorated with dozens of both creepy and goofy faces, had been set up along one side of the hall with a giant cutout of a witch riding her broomstick hanging overhead. She had a crooked nose with a wart on it that looked as big as a thumb.

She looked pretty unhappy hanging there, and Laura had this odd thought that maybe she was really unhappy about having that wart, or maybe she was just unhappy because people would be staring at the wart. So maybe they should have never put something like that up because it made fun of people with warts. And maybe that was just being "politically correct", which was a phrase Laura heard all the time but she'd never really understood what it meant.

Her dad said it meant that sometimes people were just so careful about everybody's feelings that it was hard to have a normal sense of humor anymore—people were encouraged to be too sensitive about everything. Her mom said there was nothing wrong with trying not to hurt other people's feelings, that not being able to tell certain jokes was a small price to pay for someone's happiness. Laura thought that both of these opinions sounded true, so how was she supposed to know what to think?

At their table the band boosters were selling orange-iced cupcakes with a white skull design in the center. Of course—the band boosters were always selling something. She kind of liked the band—they were good—but didn't they have enough money by now for every trip, instrument, and uniform change imaginable?

And who could eat a cupcake this early in the morning? She loved cupcakes, but she wasn't at all tempted. Maybe later.

There were candles everywhere—cat-shaped and wolf-shaped, and half-melted, old and yellowed—but of course none were lit because Principal Figg would never allow such a thing. Demonic cats, rats, bats, even bunnies! Dozens of grizzly, loopy, screaming, scary skulls!

A tall skinny girl walked down the hall wearing a hat that looked like a bat! She passed a picture of a big yellow crescent moon with a clown's face in the center, taped to a door.

A little boy walked by wearing a tall old-fashioned pilgrim hat bigger than his head. Piled up by the water fountain were pumpkins, skulls, and bones. On the wall above them black cats playing fiddles and flutes, black cats wearing vests and bow ties, black cats with their big tongues and teeth, singing and dancing.

Pirates appeared to be popular this year. She probably saw a dozen or more kids dressed as pirates in only the first few minutes of the school day. Lots of witches and wizards, of course, and way too many vampires. There was even a vampire wearing a cowboy hat! If they passed around a petition banning vampire costumes Laura would probably sign it.

There were a couple of pig people, and that was cool. They were holding hands, so they were probably dating. And three scarecrows of three different sizes. She saw one alligator who had to keep opening his jaws with both hands in order to talk to people. That was awkward, but she was pretty sure she'd never seen an alligator costume before, so you had to give him points for originality. It made her think of Trevor and his predicament, but he seemed to be enjoying himself, all these sights and sounds distracting him from that awful mouse head.

Each of the classrooms in the front hall was dedicated to a particular theme or idea, and it didn't surprise her at all that the very first was "Halloween Safety" in

Miss Reynolds' room. Principal Figg was all about safety. He had started before-and after school-and lunch break safety patrols and had the teachers announce the locations of the nearest emergency exits to their classrooms at the beginning of each class. Later, when Benny Cregger was goofing around and tried to pierce Tom Willet's left ear with a stapler, Principal Figg banned staplers in school. Even the teachers couldn't have staplers—they had to use paperclips. Laura figured it was a good thing Benny hadn't done anything dumb with paperclips. Yet.

Actually, the school did feel a lot safer under Principal Figg, but sometimes she missed having her little red stapler.

Miss Reynolds gave a short talk on safety to each new group passing through her classroom while student volunteers handed out glow-in-the-dark sticks and armbands, as well as reflective treat bags to anyone who wanted them.

"Although it's tempting to run across the street from house to house, you should always use the provided crosswalks, especially when trick-or-treating. Wearing a mask impairs your vision and drivers may be distracted by all the costumes and additional noise and activity during this holiday." She paused, and glanced at Principal Figg who stood at the back of the room. "You will want to have any of the treats you've collected examined carefully by your parents before you eat them. Or take them to one of our local urgent care clinics who are volunteering a free X-ray service. A list of those facilities is taped by the classroom door. I—I wouldn't attempt snacking on your treats before having their safety verified."

Some of the kids snickered at this. Who could resist snacking while trick-or-treating?

"It's just that razor blades and needles—that sort of thing—have been found in candy in the past. It's highly unlikely this will happen to you, but you can't be too careful."

Laura could tell that Miss Reynolds wasn't entirely happy with what she was saying—maybe she and Principal Figg had disagreed on the safety approach. Laura had read a lot about this. Almost all those cases had turned out to be kids putting dangerous stuff in their candy to get noticed, or, and it was terrible to think about, a parent or other close relative who had tried to hurt the kid or create some attention and sympathy. But that was the kind of thing you didn't usually talk about in school, what some crazy parents did. She thought she understood why. They didn't want to traumatize kids. And she'd never told Trevor about what she'd read either—he would probably freak out.

Trevor hadn't left her side. He was sitting in the next seat, listening carefully for once—maybe he was so scared that anything at all about safety comforted him. That was okay today—there weren't the usual classes and everybody was moving around the school all mixed together. Normally she'd find it a little annoying, spending every moment with her little brother, but not today—until he got that stupid mask off she wanted to keep him close.

In the hall she ran into Tammy Flynn. It was her parents who were going to be throwing that special party for her class that night. Of course there was no way she could go now—she had to be with Trevor until midnight to get him through this.

Tammy was dressed in a shirt that had "Property of the County Jail" stenciled on the back and the words "What Are You Looking At?" handwritten on the front in red lipstick. She had a fake cigarette hanging out of the corner of her mouth and her hair was all greased back. Which was all kind of hilarious since she was probably the nicest kid in school. Not that smoking meant you weren't nice or that people in jail didn't have any good qualities—this wasn't the fifties after all—but Halloween costumes weren't meant to be subtle.

"Hey, Laura! Why no costume?" Tammy asked.

Laura had run out of the house without putting on her costume that morning. She'd been anxious to get Trevor down to the school before their parents got any more suspicious than they probably already were, and worrying over her own costume would have been just too much to deal with. "I thought I'd just save it for tonight, let it be a surprise. The main event, you know?"

"You are coming tonight, aren't you?" Tammy asked, although it was hard for her to talk with that fake cigarette in her mouth. "It's going to be great."

"Oh, I know it will be, but I have to be with Trevor tonight."

Tammy looked down at Trevor, as if noticing him for the first time. "Oh, hi Trevor. Cool mask." Trevor shook his head no, which wasn't suspicious at all of course, but Tammy didn't seem to notice. "Well he can come too."

"I thought it was only for kids in our class."

"Oh, I know. But Jamie has to watch her little sister, and Robert has these little twin brothers he's supposed to take around. So Mom and I figured a few of the little brothers and sisters can come too. Mom'll watch them. No prob."

"Wow, Tammy. That's great."

"Good, I'll see you both there, then." She trotted off.

Trevor pulled her close and whispered, "What if somebody finds out?" The mouse snout kept bumping into her face because Trevor didn't know how to judge the distance.

"They won't," she whispered back. "Who would ever imagine that was even possible? This is a *good* thing, Trevor. It'll help us fill the time until that mask lets go of you."

She thought Mr. Jennings' room was a lot more interesting. He had everybody sit in chairs in the middle of the room. Along the sides of the room hung these figures made out of gauze and cotton and paper. They were like ghosts, she guessed, spirits, but they'd all been made a little differently. The cotton was stuffed into the heads for the most part, but here and there it had been sewn in clumps to the gauze, trailing away like maybe rotting ghost flesh.

Sometimes little bits of hair dangled from the heads and sometimes not. And sometimes what hung loose was just a little strip of cloth, like a piece of shirt or dress they might have worn when they were alive. Some had very basic faces—a blurry smudge for an eye, a nose, a mouth—and some had no faces at all.

Several of these spectral figures were attached to this giant windmill contraption fixed to the ceiling. Mr. Jennings' room had always had a huge old fan in the center of the ceiling, and now the windmill frame had been attached to it, and with clothesline running between the arms, and spooky figures were hanging from those lines.

Mr. Jennings came into the room with an old book open in his hands. He was dressed up in this crude costume that was basically just overalls with bunches of straw sticking out of the sleeves and pockets. A rough mask made out of white papier-mâché covered part of his face. It wasn't made very well but Laura kind of had the feeling it wasn't supposed to look all that professional. It was supposed to look homemade. Mr. Jennings kind of looked like a scarecrow, but she thought he actually represented something a lot more mysterious than that. Whatever he was supposed to be, he made her feel uneasy.

He cleared his throat and began reading. "This is the day of Samhain, the ancient Celtic festival, and the beginning of Winter. This is the eve of the day when those who have died this year return to possess the bodies of the living." At that point one of the students jiggled the dial on the fan control. The ghostly figures swayed back and forth and eerie, windy music began to play. "So on this eve the people will dress up in the most terrifying garb to scare these spirits away."

Several students marched into the room dressed up in primitive costumes similar to Mr. Jennings'. They had straw glued to their ragged clothes and their masks were even simpler and cruder than his, and Laura thought that in their way they were some of the scariest masks she'd ever seen because who would wear such a clumsy mask unless they really had to, unless there was something terribly wrong with their brains? Apparently Trevor thought so too—she could feel him pressing up close against her.

The students in their ragged costumes marched around the room, yelling and screaming things like "Go away spirits of the dead!" and "I'm gonna get you, suckuh!" at the tops of their lungs. The kid at the fan control started playing with the dial more aggressively, and the spirits would follow the marching costumes for a few steps, and then they would swing in the opposite direction, retreating as the marching students turned around and tried to scare and chase them away. It went back and forth like this for a few minutes, getting faster and faster until finally they cut off the lights and the kids in costume shouted "Boo!" Laura and Trevor practically jumped out of their seats.

It wasn't that long until lunch and in the next room kids were selling "soul cakes", little cakes people used to hand out in the old days in exchange for prayers said for the dead. But unlike the old days, these versions were rice crispy squares with raisins and cinnamon on top, five cents each. Laura bought one each for her and Trevor.

It was at this point that Trevor's mask started misbehaving.

A soul! a soul! a soul-cake!
  Please good Missus, a soul-cake!
  An apple, a pear, a plum or a cherry,
  Any good thing to make us all merry,
  One for Peter, two for Paul,
  Three for Him who made us all.

Children singing the night away. Children singing to keep their fears at bay. Do they even know what they're singing or why? We all need good thoughts, good wishes, and especially for the dead. Where has grandmother gone? Where have they all gone? Why aren't all the neighborhoods empty? How can it be that people we have known and loved suddenly aren't there at all? Think about them when you eat this sweetness, this goodness. Think of them who no longer have the pleasure of eating at all.

"Laura—"

Laura looked up smiling from her soul cake meal—it was kind of dry but still pretty tasty—to see Trevor, his eyes all wide and panicky down in the deep eye holes of the mask. He was spitting up pieces of soul cake everywhere. "Trevor! What are you doing?" She looked around; people were staring.

"It's not me!" he cried, and Laura realized what happened. It was the mask that had gotten the food, not Trevor. Just for a second she'd forgotten that little problem. And the mask must not have liked the soul cake because its long nose was all wrinkled and it was blowing dry bits of the stuff everywhere.

She grabbed Trevor's arm and dragged him outside and let the mask finish the little fit it was throwing. Then she brushed Trevor off. She took him over to the side of the school building under some shade trees where they could have some privacy. It was scary how much power the mask had. Every time it moved or jerked it dragged Trevor's head, and the rest of his little body, along with it. He looked like he was having a series of nervous convulsions. That couldn't be good for him.

"I—I wanted same of the soul cake," he said, voice cracking.

"I know," Laura said. "I'm sorry—I should have been paying more attention. I'll get you another one later, or we'll make us some at home. It looked pretty easy. But I'll get us lunch in a few minutes." There was a concrete bench under a tree a few yards away. She guided him to it and sat him down—the mouse head's constant movements were keeping him off balance. "You can sit on this bench and I'll get the food and bring it back. We're just lucky it's warm enough we can eat outside today."

"Yeah, real lucky, that's me," he said mournfully. "I just want to go home and hide."

"I know, Trev, but you can't. Dad took the day off work to decorate the house—I know he thinks he's doing it for us, but he's really into it in a super nerdy way, bless his heart. Besides, people will notice we're gone."

"Okay. Well, hurry. Smelling that soul cake and not being able to eat it—it's got me awfully hungry."

Laura raced over to the cafeteria where a big sign said: TODAY ONLY, FRANKENSTEINS & BLOODY BEANS, which turned out to be regular franks and beans with some tomato sauce mixed in. But the picture on the sign was pretty cool. Somebody had drawn a hotdog that looked like a stiff-legged, walking monster with a crewcut and a loopy grin on its face. She got two Styrofoam lunch trays and bought an extra Jello for Trevor—cherry, his favorite.

But when she got back to the bench Trevor wasn't there. "Trevor!" she yelled, looking around. She put the trays down on the bench and began searching the grounds. There was a path of flattened grass leading off into a bunch of bushes a few feet away. "Trevor?" She followed them.

She thought she heard a squirrel chattering in distress as she passed through the bushes. It was obviously angry, upset, something, with all that noise it was making. She walked past the last bush into a little clearing which had a tree in the middle. Trevor was lying face down near the tree, drag marks like train tracks trailing behind him. "Trevor!" The mouse head was rocking violently back and forth when she ran up to him. She saw that the mouth of the mask (No way would Trevor be doing this on purpose!) was clamped down on the tail of a frenzied squirrel!

"Trevor, are you okay?" But of course he couldn't

say anything—his mouth, or rather the mask's mouth, was full. The squirrel batted aggressively at the mouse head, trying to free itself. Trevor's hands were smeared with dirt and grass stains from his struggle to stop the mouse head from dragging him along. She was grateful, at least, that it hadn't broken his neck. What in the world was she going to do?

She looked around for something to use. A green hose like a big fat snake lay nearby. She followed it around the tree and found the open end. Picking it up, she yanked it as hard as she could.

The hose tightened and she saw where it was attached to the spigot on the side of the building. She ran over and turned the water on. When she got back it was gushing water. She dragged it over to Trevor and stopped, thinking about how much he hated getting wet, but what choice did she have? She wedged her thumb partway over the opening to force a good hard spray and pointed it at Trevor, trying to focus it on where the mouse head held tight to the squirrel's tail.

Trevor squawked, the squirrel squawked, and the mouse head let go of the tail, coughing and spitting. The squirrel dashed up the tree. Laura dropped the hose and ran over to help Trevor up.

He stood, dripping and shaking, his shoulders slumped. He could have gotten a lot wetter, she supposed, but he was still awfully wet. "Oh, Trevor," she said in sympathy. "I'm sorry."

"The… my head went after something the squirrel had. Then it—it just went after the squirrel. Do squirrels taste good? I bet—" He sniffed. "They don't. I bet they taste like an old rotten shoe!"

"Are you hurt?"

"Don't—think so. I put my hands down to crawl, like a big lizard? So it didn't hurt my neck."

"That was pretty smart, Trev."

"Thanks. Thanks." He raised his head, and his eyes and the mask's eyes lined up, looking at her, both of them looking at her, water dripping onto Trevor's clothes, and it was all just too awful. "Could we eat now?"

A few minutes later they were eating on the bench together. Laura pulled the brush out of her backpack, and when they sat down together she quickly jammed the brush into the mask's mouth to keep it open so that Trevor could eat. She was getting the hang of it now, but this was something she really didn't want to get used to.

Trevor was making her wet, sitting so close, but she wasn't about to complain. When she'd seen him lying there in the grass with the squirrel in the mask's mouth she'd been terrified—he could have been really hurt.

"It's pretty good with all that tomato sauce," he said softly.

She smiled. "Yeah—they should fix it this way all the time."

"We should tell Mom. She might like to make it this way."

"Yeah, yeah. Good idea."

They were quiet for a while, and then Trevor said, "We should go sit in the sun for a few minutes. I want to dry out before we go back inside."

Laura just nodded and didn't say anything. She was afraid she was going to cry.

*T*rick or treat,
   smell my feet,
give us something good to eat,
a penny or a sweet
we'd like from you.
We'll sing a song,
tell a joke if you do.

After lunch the gym filled quickly with the teachers ushering the kids inside and into their chairs. Principal Figg watched, looking at every face as if he knew what secrets they had, what mischief they were up to, and

Laura was just positive that he would know instantly if anybody was missing. His presentation on "Tricks" was mandatory for everyone in school.

A lot of the kids made fun of Principal Figg because of the way he acted and the way he looked. He was older than most of the teachers—Tammy said he'd taught her mother, but that just seemed like crazy talk. How was it possible? He wore an old-fashioned suit every day, and usually a fancy vest of some kind. Laura didn't know anyone else who actually wore a vest outside of weddings or the movies. It made him look like he was from another time, especially with those little glasses of his with the round lenses that kept slipping down to the end of his nose. And he was almost bald. He had a little bit of fuzz on the back of his head that looked so soft and fluffy it was almost like chick fuzz, so fluffy you might want to pet it, if that weren't such a weird thing to do, petting the back of your principal's head.

She wondered how he'd react. Could he expel you for something like that?

He had some old-fashioned opinions, or at least everybody said so. Laura wasn't so sure. Maybe it was just because of the way he looked—he looked like it was Halloween for him all the time and that he wore a costume every day—even his shiny skin made it look like he was wearing some kind of mask. So looking like that, everything he said sounded a little, well, too serious.

Principal Figg confused her, maybe because he'd taught her that you didn't have to like the way someone looked to agree with them and that sometimes you could absolutely love the way someone looked, only to figure out maybe too late they were talking nonsense.

"'Tricks,' as people call them, 'vandalism' if we're telling the truth, is America's own original contribution to the Halloween tradition. That's nothing to take pride in." Principal Figg looked down at his notes and his little glasses almost fell off his nose. Laura heard a snicker. "It began in the 1930s, when children started asking for treats as a bribe to prevent tricks. We have other names for that immoral practice, children, 'extortion' being one. Some Halloweens they actually had rioting in the streets. Now, thankfully we don't see much of that sort of thing on Halloween, except perhaps in some college towns." He sniffed loudly. "But that doesn't mean we've entirely escaped those days. I have some figures for you." He sniffed again.

Trevor stirred restlessly beside her. "Someone should blow his nose," he said.

"Psst, Trevor!" Laura looked around, her face warm. But Trevor sat gazing ahead as if nothing had happened.

The principal shook the papers in his hand hard, as if he overheard. "Just looking at our big neighbor to the north, Halloween vandalism costs the residents, merchants, and the city of New York over $1 million each year in cleanup and repair bills. It's gotten so bad they've had to ask the stores not to sell eggs and shaving cream to minors during Halloween week."

"But shaving cream tastes terrible with eggs," Trevor said, a little more loudly this time. Off to their right, Laura heard someone giggle. She tugged on Trevor's arm. "Trevor, be quiet! What's wrong with you?"

He turned his head to look up at her, his eyes wide and white as milk. "It's the mouse head again," he whispered.

Laura looked more closely at the mask. The mouse head wore a huge grin full of giant teeth.

"Now, I'm not saying you shouldn't have fun out there," Mr. Figgs continued. "I'm very much in favor of fun." Snickers sprinkled through the assembled students like rain. "Good, clean, wholesome, harmless fun. But taking a cow up an elevator into an office building, as happened in this city last year, is far from good, clean fun. Especially for the cow and those who had to clean up after it."

"I hear it would only give buttermilk after that night," the mouse head said. Laura was sure this time— she'd seen the mouth move. This mask was a talker! The voice was quite a bit like Trevor's, but if she thought about it, it was higher- pitched and very annoying.

Principal Figg paused and stared at the students. It seemed to Laura as if he was looking into the soul of each one of them, and would know instantly if any of them were hiding anything. He stopped when he came to her and pointed. She tried to sink down in her seat. "Benny Cregger. I heard that. I suppose you think you're clever. Come see me after assembly, please." Benny was seated a few rows directly behind her. She heard a mumbled, "Aw, man," perhaps Benny's most frequently used phrase. But it really wasn't fair to blame him for something the mouse head said. She'd have to make it right, but how could she do that?

After the assembly there were pumpkin carving competitions in several of the rooms using safety knives and spoons for carving tools. There was lots of noise and laughing and intense, focused carving, which probably helped distract people from Trevor's obviously misbehaving mouse head. Or maybe they thought it was just a really neat, flexible mask capable of lots of different expressions.

In any case, if the mouse head liked someone's carving job it would lick its own face with an impossibly long, pale pink tongue. But if the mouse head didn't like what they had done it would make the most horrible of faces, like it had been poisoned by some bad cheese or something. Laura tried to distract it by demonstrating to Trevor how you had to be careful to cut out the top of the pumpkin at an inward pointing angle if you didn't want the cap to fall inside the pumpkin after hollowing it out (a process which various boys insisted on referring to, rudely, as "gutting the pumpkin"). And if you cut a notch in the cap it not only provided a chimney for the smoke to escape but it also helped supply oxygen to feed the flame.

The teacher brought in a pumpkin that had been "professionally carved". It was a true work of art showing a cabin in the woods with a fire in the fireplace, smoke coming out of the chimney, and a little girl's face in the window. It was really quite beautiful and Laura had no idea how it might have been carved so intricately, but she actually found the crudely carved pumpkins of the students to be lots scarier.

It was all over school by now that Benny Cregger had been suspended. It seemed that when he sat down in front of the principal some cherry bombs fell out of his pocket. So Laura didn't have to feel guilty about Trevor's mouse head getting Benny into trouble after all.

The mouse head raised its long snout, sniffed the air, and led Trevor into the next classroom. Laura didn't have much choice except to follow.

Once inside they were surrounded by clowns. Oh great, the Clown Room, full of absolutely-too-many fake, up-to-no-good smiles. Because anybody who smiled that much had to be up to no good.

Miss Wilson suggested that everybody slip off their masks and practice using the clown makeup to create their own, individual clown "persona". Of course this made Laura panic for Trevor, but he just started putting the clown makeup on top of his mouse head and everybody was so amused Miss Wilson said it was okay, Trevor would be their "very first mouse clown".

The final activity of the day was the costume parade and contest. All classes were dismissed, and some kids who weren't much into costumes were actually going home rather than staying for the celebration. When Laura found this out she grabbed Trevor and said, "This is great. We'll go on home, you'll stay in your room until dinner, 'preparing' to go out, or whatever, we'll make it through dinner with the folks somehow, and then it's out trick-or-treating, staying out of trouble until midnight. Piece of cake, right?"

The mouse head, or Trevor—she was beginning to get them a little confused—just stared at her mournfully and said in Trevor's little voice, "but I wanted to stay for the parade! I've been looking forward to it for months, Lauraaaah!" Was he saying her name sarcastically? She thought he might be. Was this just the stress, or that sarcastic mouse head talking?

But before she could figure that out the mouse head swiveled around and leaned toward the gym where the parade was being held and began to move in that direction, dragging Trevor along with it. This was awkward because Trevor's body had been pointed in the opposite direction, so when the mouse head took charge Trevor had to scramble to his feet and reposition his body so that he didn't sprain his neck. It was pretty scary to watch. Laura didn't have any choice but to follow.

She was having a hard time deciding whether she should be annoyed with Trevor, fearful for him, or both. She didn't think he could help it, with that mouse head in control, but maybe this was the way he secretly wanted to be. Should you judge somebody because of their secret wishes? People wished, or imagined, all kinds of weird things, and the whole world would be in a lot of trouble if those wishes came true.

And sometimes things happen that make you say things you wouldn't normally say. Like sometimes when Laura had to get up early in the morning and she'd be cranky and she'd say harsh things she didn't really mean (what her mom called "getting up on the wrong side of the bed"). But that wasn't true, was it? Because she'd meant it when she said it. It was just that—at that very moment—she wasn't concerned about hurting anyone's feelings. The same thing might happen if she were hungry, or if she had a headache, or even if she just had a cold which made her sound funny, which made her feel as if she were an entirely different person. Words and opinions came out of her mouth that she didn't even know she knew, or had.

But did that make it okay? How much should you blame a person for what they said?

Sometimes it seemed people had all these little packages of words and ideas and opinions waiting to be expressed that they kept hidden away in pockets and drawers or maybe just tucked behind their ears. And some things made those packages explode—a lack of sleep or an illness or a mood or maybe just going into an internet chat room. They were like little bombs. Booby traps. And Laura didn't think you could just excuse them, like you'd had an accident and said "oops."

It was chaos inside the gym. Teachers were ordering costumed kids from the various classes to line up and get ready to start, but absolutely no one was listening. Vampires and cowboys and aliens and kitty cats stood around talking and laughing and being just generally loud and way too annoying. Big Birds and TV stars and presidents and robots grabbed at each other and argued and pushed ahead to the front of the line. Trying to catch up to Trevor and keep him out of trouble, she ran into the most obnoxious Abraham Lincoln she'd ever met. He kept sticking his gross-looking fake beard into the faces of every girl who passed and asked, "So, got a kiss for Honest Abe?"

She had no idea who he really was, but figured he

was one of those boys who couldn't even say two words to a girl without that mask on.

Jenny Carter kicked him right in his skinny Lincoln Log legs, and Laura didn't think his reaction was very presidential at all.

Trevor had wandered away again—wouldn't he ever learn?—and she walked through the maze of fantastic and less-than-fantastic creatures looking for him. "Hey, Laura!" someone in a long robe and a dog's head said. "Why don't you join the parade?"

She stared at the figure. "Who are you under that get-up?"

"That's for me to know and you to find out," the dog's head said in a kind of high-pitched voice Laura didn't recognize. In fact she couldn't even tell if the voice was male or female.

"Can't you see?" she replied. "I'm not wearing a costume."

"Oh, but that's a great costume!" a nearby figure in a cat's head and an ugly old bathrobe made a growling noise. "You should walk in the costume parade with that on for sure!" She didn't recognize this person either. She thought this one was probably a girl, but she couldn't be absolutely sure.

The situation was making her uncomfortable. It was fun trying to guess who all the costumed people were, but when they were messing with you, teasing you, that wasn't much fun at all. "Trevor? Trevor!" She raised her voice and walked around the room.

A monster with two heads jumped out at her screaming "bloody murder!" *In real life did anyone ever actually scream "bloody murder"?* But it wasn't too scary: One of the heads wore glasses. "Oh, hi Frank," Laura said, trying to sound bored.

One of the monster's heads frowned. "How'd you know it was me?" The monster reached up and stroked the other, fake head absentmindedly. It was shiny green and covered with big pink sores.

"Frank, I've known you all my life. Too long," Laura said.

"Bet you say that to all the monsters," he mumbled. "So what are you gonna be this year? A princess *or* a cheerleader? Or are you really going to be *daring* this time and go as an *airline stewardess*?"

"Very funny. I did get a mask; I just didn't want to wear it to school. Maybe you'll see it tonight, if I don't avoid you."

"Hey now. I know you're crazy about me."

"You're the one who's crazy, Frank," she replied, pushing past him, her eyes only interested in finding her brother.

She found him in a corner facing the wall. He was trying to pull the mouse head off, pressing it against the wall and pushing, apparently thinking that would help. She put her hand on his shoulder. "Trevor, you can't get it off. You'll just have to wait until midnight."

He shrugged off her hand. "It's hot, Laura! And it's itchy! It's annoying me!"

"I'm sure it is. It's supposed to be cooler tonight—that'll probably help a lot."

"And it's always thinking." He turned around. She almost couldn't see his tiny little eyes at the bottom of the eyeholes. It was like looking into a deep well for a marble or something.

"Trevor. *What?* What does that mean?"

"I can hear it thinking! It's all about being hungry, and eating, and wishing its teeth were sharper so that maybe—"

But then the music for the parade started up. It was like the music you heard at the circus, kind of happy, but it was played so badly by a few musicians from the student band she wanted to cover her ears. They started, stopped, and re-started again, as if they were wounded, dragging their instruments on the ground. It just sounded creepy and weird.

"What are you two doing here?" Mrs. Carter, the English teacher, glowered down at them, looking gigantic and threatening in her black witch costume.

"Oh, hello, Mrs. Carter—I was just helping Trevor get ready—"

"You don't belong here—you're not in costume!" Mrs. Carter said, pointing. Laura hated being pointed at. "I don't know who you think you are?"

"Remember, I'm your neighbor. We live on the same street," Laura replied. Mrs. Carter was married to Mr. Carter, the neighbor who never smiled and was always complaining about kids jumping into his leaf piles. Some couples were just made for each other, Laura guessed.

"Don't talk back to me, Laura."

"Sorry—I didn't mean to say it like that." She had been disrespectful, but Laura didn't like people who could never be nice to others. She couldn't respect that.

"You just—" Mrs. Harris began, but the mass of students was moving. She turned around in agitation. "Wait! No, go on!" she yelled and left, walking stiff-legged toward the main gym entrance.

"Is Mrs. Carter really a witch?" Trevor asked.

"No," Laura replied. "Sometimes she just acts like one."

As the paraders rushed out of the gym to start marching in the hall, the mouse head swiveled, grinned, and dragged Trevor out after them, his arms waving. Laura started to give chase but an adult's arm stopped her.

She looked up—it was Mr. Mac the wrestling instructor. He wore a bright pink mohawk wig taped to his bald head and a pirate patch over his left eye. "Sorry, kid. Costumes only."

"But my brother—"

"No problem. You can take that other door into the hall to watch him."

Laura did as she was told. The door took her around to the side where she came out into the hall a few yards ahead of the costume parade. Other students lined the corridor waiting for the parade to come around the corner. Kids pointed, and she could hear others hooting and hollering at whatever they were seeing, so she knew the parade was close by.

Brian Willis came around the corner leading the parade. That was usually a dead giveaway that the teachers in charge actually liked his costume best for some reason. But his outfit was so busy-looking Laura wasn't sure at first what he was actually supposed to be. He had taken eight long streamers of different-colored cloth and sewn an old glove to the end of each one. Then he had attached the eight streamers to an old black sweatshirt. Laura finally figured out he was dressed up as some sort of big spider. He also wore an old pair of his dad's glasses with the lenses removed. Brian had glued giant artificial eyelashes all around the frames, making two very hairy eye holes. He also wore a cheap pair of plastic vampire teeth. He was the unscariest, funniest looking spider she'd ever seen, sort of like a clown spider, if spiders had their own clowns.

Laura thought Connie James marching behind him actually had a better costume. She was a fat crocodile, like the one that ate Captain Hook, carrying a giant ticking clock in her arms. She'd made a neat stuffed crocodile tail that swept the floor back and forth as she walked. She smiled at Laura as she passed, grinning—well—like a crocodile.

Following up the crocodile there was a cluster of the smallest kids, shoved near the front of the line. And she did mean cluster—they were shuffling along tightly packed together for security, looking shy and nervous, as if they were afraid of their own costumes. They all had these store-bought outfits that were basically dresses with characters' images printed on the front—Casper, Spiderman, and a few Disney characters—with cheap plastic masks to match. She'd seen how Miss Walker, the math teacher, recruited them—she just grabbed them out of the hall at random asking them, "Do you want to be in the parade?" without bothering to hear their answer. It was like she had this quota of cute little kids to fill. Most of them obviously didn't want to be there, with everybody looking at them and laughing. Sometimes adults could be pretty dense, especially when they were in a hurry.

At that point there was an explosion of obnoxious sound behind them. Laura figured the next costumed characters would be a bunch of fat honking geese. Some of the little kids looked behind them, then scattered in terror, squealing. And then there came her brother Trevor, or rather that terrible mouse, or rather Trevor trapped inside that terrible mouse head, grinning ear-to-ear, in fact grinning so hugely she could see Trevor's pale face looking out from between the mouse head's goofy crooked teeth.

The mouse head looked even bigger than it had a few minutes ago. *Was it growing?* Mouse rocked his giant swollen head back and forth on Trevor's narrow little neck, and when it got close enough to the students standing along the hall it snapped at them, sometimes letting an impossibly long and ghostly pale tongue escape its mouth and try to lick them. When the tongue did make contact—which it did in the case of poor, trembling Margaret Gomez—it made a big sucking sound like water going down the kitchen sink. Margaret was crying, her cheek all wet and slimy.

A bunch of kids who'd been licked this way were coming up fast behind Trevor/mouse, who was now picking up speed, still grinning, but glancing behind him now and then to see how close his pursuers were. They were all well past Laura by the time she'd figured out exactly what was going on, and the hall was full of shouting, and laughing (if you weren't one of the victims) students.

The parade, with Trevor/mouse at the head of it, was now headed back toward the front door of the school, and now that classes had been dismissed for the day they'd have no trouble leaving the school grounds. Laura imagined all those kids following Trevor/mouse back to the house, where he'd be hiding in his bedroom while an angry mob shouted from their front yard, waving their torches and demanding justice, while Mom clutched the kitchen phone frantically calling the police.

Laura dashed back through the gym and out the side door that led to the baseball field, running around the side of the building to the front where, sure enough, kids were streaming off the campus in pursuit of the now-distant mouse-faced monster, stopping traffic and causing what Principal Figg would call "a general disruption." In fact she hoped the principal wasn't watching—he'd have a heart attack over the number of obvious safety violations.

The bushes by the front entrance rustled violently, scratching her arm. She jumped away. Trevor/mouse rolled out of the bushes onto the ground, flat on his back. "They didn't see me jump into the bushes!" he said breathlessly. "Laura, they were so mad!" His voice sounded frightened, but the mouse head continued to grin that crazy grin.

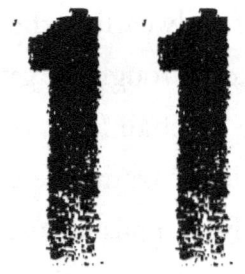

A ll the excitement when they begin the night! They've
got the best costume ever, and a brand-new empty bag
(or pillowcase, or store-bought orange bucket) all hungry for
treats. Ravenous even! Can a treat bag have an appetite?
Why not! They're out to score the biggest treat haul ever in
the entire history of Halloween, and it doesn't matter if they
can't eat it all, if they end up giving away half of it, or even
if they find it stashed under their bed during the middle of
the hottest summer with bugs crawling in it and their mother
makes them throw it out! Halloween isn't about getting
enough—no way! It's all about getting too much!

Mom made hamburgers and French fries for an early dinner, one of their all-time favorite meals. Laura asked for the early meal so that they could "get to the main event", which sounded lame, but those were the words that had come out of her mouth. She figured the sooner they got out of the house the less likely her parents would figure something was odder than odd about Trevor's mask. Trevor sat in front of his plate miserably, the mouse head (now calm, and thank goodness not grinning) weighing him down. He looked like he couldn't even raise his swollen head.

But at least he was eating. Trevor figured out that if he brought his food up to the mouse head quickly enough, the mask's mouth didn't try to steal it. The lips on the mask only moved a tiny bit. You had to be watching very closely to see it—it looked weird, like you were seeing something strange, but you really couldn't be sure. Mom and Dad stared at Trevor from time to time with puzzled looks on their faces, but they didn't say anything. They had no idea what they were seeing.

After dinner Laura and Trevor went upstairs to get ready. All Trevor did, all he could do really, was change into another set of regular clothes. He didn't even bother to find something brown or more mouse-like. Laura was glad he at least had fresh clothes in his closet. His school clothes were all sweaty, from stress she guessed, and they stank. Actually, they smelled like a trunk they used to have in the basement that the field mice had gotten into. All stale smells and wild animal stinky. She wondered if the inside of Trevor's mask smelled something like that, and she felt even sorrier for him.

She brought him another smoothie she'd made. He sucked on the straw eagerly, the mouse head not bothering him—maybe it had already had enough of Trevor's food to satisfy it temporarily.

"Thanks," he said, sounding relieved.

"Do you still feel like you're starving?"

"Not so much," he replied. "The mask let me have a little of the burger and fries. Maybe it knows it has to keep my strength up so I can do whatever it plans."

She shivered a little when Trevor said plans. "Maybe it doesn't have any plans. Maybe it does what a mouse would do. I don't think mice are big planners."

"Maybe," he said and burped loudly. Laura couldn't tell if it was a Trevor burp or a mouse head burp.

Their mom gave a little gasp when she saw Laura in her mask. With all the hassles over Trevor's mask Laura had forgotten how much her own resembled her mother. Her dad gave her a little hug. "You look beautiful, sweetheart," he said, which he'd said before, but of course now it was partly because of her mask and who she looked like. Her mom hugged her too, but didn't say anything. She did look a little emotional, though. Was it because of the resemblance, or because it made Laura look grown up?

Dad asked her and Trevor to stand in the archway between the living room and dining room while he took their picture. "We've got to preserve the moment!" he exclaimed dorkily. He was always saying that. He took three or four because sometimes he messed up. He even asked them to smile, which made Laura giggle a little, because who could tell if they were smiling or not with their masks on?

Laura kept glancing over at Trevor. The mouse head was trembling, as if it was trying to do something crazy. Of course, it apparently loved attention, so it was likely to act up when there was a camera around. Luckily their dad said "all done" before anything weird happened.

Laura almost didn't hear her mother ordering them to have fun when they walked out the door. For some reason it made her stop and turn around. She ran back to her mom and gave her a big hug.

It was still pretty early, and not really dark yet, so it was mostly the smallest kids out with their parents trick-or-treating at this hour. There were young couples out carrying their babies, who Laura had to admit were quite cute dressed up as pumpkins, or kittens, or angels. She saw one baby in some sort of caterpillar suit who appeared to be sleeping the whole time. All very, very cute. But she really didn't quite see the point. The babies certainly had no clue what was going on, or what they were wearing, and the candy they were collecting—the parents would be eating that, surely, but adults were supposed to know better than to eat all that junk. Were they just showing the neighbors how cute their new baby was? Was that the purpose? Laura guessed so, but she wasn't a parent, maybe that's why she just didn't get it. Did other kids her age think about this stuff?

She and Trevor didn't go up to any houses the first half hour or so. It would have felt weird to compete with those parents with their babies and their real little kids. So they just walked, and checked things out. The mouse head was calm for now, letting Trevor be in charge.

They came across a robot leaning against a lamp post, looking at his watch impatiently. It was Frank—Laura could tell because of the red and yellow tennis shoes. No one else in school, or probably anywhere else in the world, had tennis shoes like that. Frank was always coming up with unique clothing items. His dad worked for a designer. "Neat costume, Frank," Trevor said once they got there.

"What? How'd you know?"

Laura pointed at his shoes and said. "Who else has those tennis shoes? You're wearing a different costume from that two- headed thing you had on at school. What's up with that?"

"Someone ran into my other head at the riot or what-ever that was that happened at the school. Broke it off, neck and all, and somebody stepped on the face. What happened there anyway? Somebody said some kid in a mouse mask—Trevor? You're wearing a mouse mask. Do you know what they're talking about?"

"He was sick most of the day," Laura answered hast-ily. "Didn't they say it was a rat mask? That's what I heard." She was glad she was wearing her mask—she was sure she was blushing fiercely because of the lie.

"Yeah," Trevor said. "I ate one of those orange

cupcakes they were selling. Made me sick. I was in the bathroom most of the day."

Laura frowned, nodding. "Oh yeah, pretty gross," she added.

"Oh," Frank replied. "Thanks bunches for telling me."

He shook his robot box head, which was loose and flopped around his neck. The head looked a lot like a television set. In fact, it had an old "rabbit ears" TV antenna taped to the top of the box, and thin, see-through cloth covered the square hole in the front to make a screen. TV-head Frank stared at Laura for a while, the box nodding up and down as if it were scanning or X- raying her or something. Frank often made Laura feel uncomfortable, but this year his costumes—both of them— made it worse. "So what are you supposed to be?" he finally asked her.

Laura hesitated. She hadn't really thought much about who, or what to call herself this year. "I'm kind of like a Laura from another time. Myself in the future, or from another dimension, kind of, something like that."

"You look a little like a ghost. Laura's ghost."

"Gee thanks," she said sarcastically. "I always wanted to look dead."

"No, I didn't mean like that. You look grown up, and

kind of romantic. Beautiful but ghostly." Frank said this softly, like he wanted just her to hear.

"Oh." She was genuinely surprised. "Thanks, Frank. That was a really nice thing to say."

"Welcome," he replied, his robot head turning slightly away from her, as if embarrassed.

"Can we go now?" Trevor asked anxiously. "It's getting dark."

"Well, I gotta meet some people anyway," Frank said. "Are you going to the party later?"

Laura looked down at Trevor. "I'm going to try. Maybe I'll see you there."

"Yeah—that would be great. See ya." It looked like Frank was trying to stand up straight and leave with some kind of dignity. Of course that was impossible in that silly costume. His box head kept swiveling around so he couldn't see well, so that when he turned around he clanked his head against the lamppost. Laura heard him swearing under his breath—he probably didn't know she could hear him. Sometimes people imagined they were soundproof when they put on a disguise, however flimsy.

His TV antenna fell off. Laura scooped it up and handed it back to him. "Thank you," he mumbled, and limped away holding his head—both his robot head and his real head.

She looked down at Trevor. "Why were you being so rude?"

"Didn't mean to," he said sullenly. "But Frank was really annoying the mouse head. I could tell."

"Annoying him? What are you talking about?"

"Every time Frank said something the mouse thoughts got all staticky—like if you're watching TV and the antenna disconnects. It was thinking it wanted to rip open that cardboard box of his and eat whatever treats were hiding inside."

"Trevor! That's terrible!"

"Hey—it wasn't my idea. This mouse head has ideas of its own—I'm just along for the ride. I wouldn't want to hurt Frank. I always thought he was cool."

And I didn't, she thought, feeling a little guilty.

"Could we start trick-or-treating, Laura? Midnight is an awfully long time away. I don't want to just wait around—I'll be so bored!"

"Okay. You're right. But if you start feeling—I don't know-crazy, destructive, or just generally weird, tell me, okay?"

Laura glanced at her watch and froze. She tried to

control her facial expression—she didn't want to worry him. But the watch was acting strangely—the numbers rolling forward, then rolling backwards. But still, no problem. They would be passing lots of kids with watches. She'd just ask for the time. She could do this.

By now a lot of the smaller kids (except for Trevor, of course,) were already on their way home, following their parents down the sidewalks, whining, wanting to be carried, crying about how they were so tired, dragging their treat bags on the ground behind them, and getting all upset and dramatic if candy spilled out as a result. Laura wasn't sure she'd ever have kids, but thought she might, and wondered if she could get away with not ever telling them about Halloween.

Some of the little kids had pretty interesting costumes, expensive-looking things bought for them by parents who apparently hadn't figured out yet that they didn't have to spend a fortune to keep their smaller kids happy. A number of the kids looked like little realistic stuffed animals in their soft, furry all-body suits. And she saw kids dressed as oranges and bananas, all kinds of fruits, forks and spoons, and pretty much anything you might find in a fairy tale or a Disney movie. Some of the smallest children—if she just squinted her eyes a little—looked like weird combinations of creatures, strange genetic experiments half kid and half fruit, half girl and half puppy, half human child and half stalk of celery (a very short stalk, but a stalk just the same).

She saw the usual bunch of kids dressed as hobos, with ragged clothes and some kind of dark gray makeup to make it look like they badly needed a thorough shaving and a bath. Kids had been dressing up like hobos forever, of course—her dad said he'd been a hobo once or twice. All it took were some old clothes and some dirt (or dirt-like makeup if you didn't want to actually get dirty, although Laura wasn't quite sure she understood the difference. At the end of the evening you still had to wash both of them off). Dad said he had a stick with a bedroll tied to it slung over his shoulder—sometimes people called that thing a *bindlestiff*, but Dad said "bindlestiff" was actually another name for a hobo.

Either way, hobo costumes made her uncomfortable because of all the real poor people in the world. So maybe she believed in being "politically correct" just like her mom.

With the younger kids sometimes it was obvious that the costume was all their parents' idea. This night she saw both a walking haystack and a talking tree, and someone she thought was supposed to be a corn cob, but she wasn't quite sure. In all these cases it was hard for the kids to move and they had to have a parent there or an older brother or sister to guide them around because they couldn't see properly. This was just another example of parents wanting to be creative and complicating their children's fun. What kid in their right mind would want to be a tree or—really—a haystack?

She and Trevor passed a young couple who were walking quickly down the sidewalk, looking tired and—as her mother sometimes said—on their "last nerves."

The dad twisted his head around and called back, "Come on guys! It's past bedtime!"

The little boy hurrying up next looked kind of bloody at first, and Laura was alarmed. Then she saw that his costume was just bright red and lumpy with little bits of white speckled through the red. "Ugghhhh! He's supposed to be a raw hamburger!" Trevor exclaimed. "I think I'm going to throw up!"

A bun came running up behind him. "Jimmy! Wait!" the bun exclaimed on the verge of tears.

The mouse head turned suddenly and made a loud sniffing noise, its snout wrinkling up. "Trevor!" Laura cried in alarm.

"It's okay," he replied timidly. "I think it's just curious."

A tall, silky gray kitten strolled down the sidewalk, a small basket with just a few treats dangling delicately from one long paw. Laura recognized the kitten instantly as Amanda Payes, who loved all things cat related.

Amanda-the-kitten strolled up to the pair of them and started to say something. She stopped, staring at Trevor's mouse head. She tilted her head left, then tilted it right, her small pale tongue peeking out from between her lips. The cheeks of the mouse head began to swell, as if they had great gobs of food stuffed into them, and then the lips pulled back, exposing an amazing set of teeth—teeth like dozens of shiny stalactites hanging down in the opening of a cave, teeth like a collection of dangling daggers, teeth like the fiercest tiger or ancient giant Saber tooth.

Amanda made a tiny squeaking noise, just like a real kitten, turned and ran back up the sidewalk as fast as her delicate paws could carry her.

Laura was getting a pretty clear idea of what this Halloween was going to be like. "Trev, we've got to find some way to control—" But Trevor was already off and running, the mouse head apparently excited because of this kitty cat encounter. She ran after him, and her mask immediately shifted, the eye holes not lining up anymore so it was hard to see. She had to stop and adjust things. She started running again and quickly discovered that the mask made it harder to breathe. Luckily she was able to grab Trevor's arm before he got them both into trouble.

G *rab your bag and little brother's hand, drag him across the street as fast as you can! Grin and grin and grin some more, Trick-or-Treat, Trick-or-Treat, Trick-or-more! Ghosts and goblins and things that go bump, but when little brother starts howling then you'll jump!*

Everything looks a little differently when you're wearing a mask. Maybe because the eyeholes just never quite fit your eyes right, and it makes it harder to see, so that sometimes you're just seeing little pieces of things your mind tries to put together into a complete picture: the moon coming through the trees, the slices of shadow, the racing feet, the candles and flashlight, the fractured masks and costumes, all that black and orange.

Laura had been hoping maybe they could lay back a little, walk around, visit a few houses, keep things calm and low-key. If Trevor and his mouse head behaved themselves maybe they could even try going to the party, bob a few apples, have a couple of cups of punch, talk to a few friends, and walk around some more.

But Trevor had never had that much stamina. He always wanted to stay up for some special TV show or other, and he'd beg Mom and Dad to let him go way past his bedtime so that he could watch one of the milder horror movies with Laura, but he never, ever made it. In fact he'd get so worked up and exhausted over these "special shows" it practically guaranteed he'd fall asleep even before his regularly scheduled bedtime.

That's what Laura had been hoping would happen tonight. Trevor would get more and more tired and then finally he wouldn't be able to walk anymore, and then they'd have to sit down and his eyes would start fluttering, and his head would start dipping, and before she knew it he'd be fast asleep.

She had no idea exactly what was supposed to happen at midnight. Maybe the mouse head would just fall off and free Trevor's head, or maybe after that hour she could just lift it off. Or maybe it would vanish, or turn into a bunch of leaves that would drift away on the October breeze. Or maybe some guy with no head riding a big black horse would come up to them and take the mouse head away, and that mouse head would become the headless rider's new head.

The possibilities were endless.

But for now, the immediate issue was that Trevor showed absolutely no signs of fatigue—if anything he looked more energetic than she'd ever seen him. Laura was pretty sure the slow, relaxed, sleepy evening she'd imagined was not going to happen.

A young kid in a mouse costume walked by, clutching his almost full bag of treats. He didn't have any kind of mask, just the mouse body. He stared at Trevor with unmistakable envy. *Oh, if you only knew*, Laura thought.

The mouse head was quite obviously in the mood for trick-or-treating. Maybe it was in anticipation of all the candy to be had, or maybe it was a growing hunger for adventure, but the mouse head jerked solidly in the direction of the next house they came to, dragging Trevor's body awkwardly and painfully up the narrow front walk. Laura raced to catch up with him.

They ran into three little boys coming off the front porch. Laura figured they were the Thompson brothers since they were all short and fat and squealed a lot. They were all three dressed as snowballs, big fat snowballs, which, actually, Laura thought was kind of cute. Then she heard one of them gasp. Mickey Thompson, she thought.

"A giant mouse!" Mickey Thompson cried. "I hate mice!"

The mouse head swiveled toward Mickey and grinned scarily. "Ummmm, a snow cone. I love me a snow cone!" it said, in a voice completely unlike Trevor's, in fact completely unlike any voice she'd ever heard before—kind of high-pitched, like that of the cartoon mouse the mask resembled, but so loud and growly it reminded Laura more of a wolf.

A narrow pale tongue began to slowly creep out of the mouse head's mouth. Mickey Thompson, who had been scrambling down the sidewalk as fast as he could (which wasn't very fast), stopped and looked around, as if he knew something very interesting and unusual was about to happen.

Laura felt the same way, and held her breath.

The mouse head's pale tongue flicked out several

yards, unfurling like a streamer, like a wriggling snake, growing wider at the end, until it landed on the back of Mickey Thompson's snowball costume and began licking it up and down with loud wet noises.

Mickey screamed and ran away, stumbling once or twice and falling on the grass, rolling, crying out, and getting up again, running some more. He lost his treat bag and all his candy, but didn't seem to notice. But it hurt Laura to see it—she'd always been sensitive about the disappointments little kids had to suffer and wondered how she could fix this.

In the meantime the mouse head was coughing and spitting. "Cotton!" it complained. "That faker wasn't tasty at all!"

But its disgust was apparently temporary. Within seconds it had forgotten all about the incident and was pulling Trevor down the sidewalk to the next house.

A tall, skinny kid dressed all in black appeared to be floating down the sidewalk toward them. Laura thought she'd seen him around school, if the figure under the dark costume was who she thought it was. She didn't know his name—he didn't socialize much—but with his tall skinny frame and somewhat moon-shaped face he was pretty distinctive looking.

And his costume was pretty distinctive looking as well. As he got closer it looked at first as if he had no arms, but then she realized that his arms had become two of the eight spider legs that hung from the swollen spider body that covered his shoulders. He should have been the one in the school parade today representing the *arachnid* kingdom. The six other legs moved as easily and as gracefully as the ones made out of his two arms—how did he do that? And all eight looked impossibly narrow and skinny, like long crooked branches. Laura shuddered in disgust. Even the mouse head apparently found the costume creepy, wrinkling its snout and leaning so heavily away from the passing spider Trevor almost tipped over.

Then they ran into two teenage girls dressed in beautiful moth costumes. Laura thought they might actually be following the spider, an interesting switch in the usual order of things. But the spider was shy and didn't seem too interested in them.

The mouse head obviously found their appearance much more to his liking and leaned their way, sniffing loudly and (gross!) licking his lips with that skinny pale tongue. The closest moth started moving her arms back and forth, making it look as if she were rising off the sidewalk. The other one turned and stared with eyes like big swollen ping pong balls. Laura knew it was just part of the costume but it freaked her out anyway. She looked quickly away and gave Trevor a little shove in the back that got him moving again.

At the next house Trevor walked a little more slowly up the sidewalk, his mouse head looking down, his treat bag dragging on the ground behind him. Several kids came up to the porch in front of him and he just joined the back of the crowd, acting as if he wasn't quite sure what to do next.

Laura stood slightly off the side of the porch and watched as the first row of kids presented their bags and yelled "Trick or Treat" more or less simultaneously as an elderly woman opened the front door. The woman threw up her hands in mock shock and cried dramatically, "Oh, so scary!" and a little girl in the front wearing a lop-sided crown giggled. The woman went around with a basket full of candy and invited each of the kids to grab a handful as she exclaimed, "Such terrifying ghosts, goblins, and beasties!"

The next kid in line was a little boy wearing a paper airplane tied to his head with string and wearing what was probably supposed to have been a pilot's uniform but really looked more like blue pajamas. "Trigger treat!" the little boy cried.

The old woman smiled. "And so creative!" She gave him his turn at the treat bowl.

Laura thought that at least here was a kid whose parents let him pick out his own costume (she hoped), whatever the results might be. And she was surprised that given the opportunity to take whatever they wanted the kids hadn't taken advantage and gotten greedy. Obviously, this sweet old lady hadn't yet encountered any of her friends.

When it was Trevor's turn he came up slowly, head down, and mumbled out some version of "trick or treat." This was much more like the way the old Trevor would have behaved in public, but Laura held her breath, waiting for the mouse head to go berserk on the unsuspecting lady's porch. The old lady looked at the mouse head curiously, as if she'd never seen anything like it before, and of course she hadn't. Laura supposed that, as masks go, it was unusually well made, obviously so, the ears and the nose and the fur of the head real-looking, super-real looking, actually. If you stared at it long enough you imagined you could see the warmth given off it, and the lush environment it provided for fleas.

You might even imagine you could see the traces of blood vessels beneath the scalp, the way they pulsed when the head moved or when the mouse was feeling some powerful emotion.

The old lady extended her hand, apparently intent on touching, or stroking it. Laura heard herself gasp, afraid of what was about to happen.

The mouse head looked up, and although Laura couldn't see the snout from this angle, she imagined it wasn't making that hideous grin because the elderly lady remained calm. "Take what you like, dear," she said.

When Trevor didn't reach for any candy despite the woman's offer—and that was so like Trevor when dealing with adult strangers—the woman took a handful of candy and dropped it into his bag. "There you go," she said.

When Trevor turned to go without saying anything more, Laura called out, "Thank you, ma'am," the way she'd seen parents do with their shy little kids.

She hoped this meant that the mouse head was permitting Trevor to be in charge for a little while, and for the next couple of hours that seemed to be true. Trevor would go up onto the porches, either by himself or with another group of kids, and politely stand there, say the standard line, and receive his treats. After a while he even started saying "Thank you" on his own without her prompting.

There were signs now and then that the mad mouse was still in there—it hadn't gone away completely. Every once in a while he'd be standing near a particular costume—some animal, alien, or once a tall kid in a medieval outfit—and the weird grin would cross its face, sometimes with a large display of teeth, and he'd sniff, or make some other inappropriate gesture. In the case of the medieval kid dressed up as some sort of scholar holding a scroll, the mouse head ate one of the feathers in the kid's fancy cap without the kid even knowing it.

But this only happened occasionally. For the most part the mouse head behaved itself, and Laura was beginning to hope for a peaceful rest of the evening before the mask was removed at midnight.

O *ld Witch, Old Witch, she lives in a ditch,*
And combs her hair with a hickory switch.
She lives on nails and snails and flies
And if you go near she'll wobble her eyes,
Oh, she'll wobble her eyes, Oh, she'll wobble her eyes.

So much anticipation, followed by so much joy, followed by so much plain old exhaustion! Who knew fun could be so much work? Who knew that running up and down the street, screaming and singing and laughing and eating every piece of candy you can get your hands on would leave you so tired you can't even keep your eyelids up? Anybody should be able to hold their eyelids up—how much do they weigh anyway, a fourth of an ounce?

Maybe it was because she was older (but she wasn't *that* old) or because she was so stressed out watching over Trevor and worrying over him and waiting for the mouse head to just completely freak out, but Laura started getting super tired even before it was time for the party and way before their midnight deadline. Her feet dragged, her head nodded, and she was pretty sure she wasn't thinking too straight (was that a raccoon wearing a dress walking by?) and she couldn't imagine lasting for more than a few minutes longer. Was it possible for a teenage girl to die of exhaustion in America?

Laura was desperately trying to keep up with Trevor, or the mouse head that was steering a sleepy-eyed, exhausted Trevor wherever it wanted to go, when a figure in a familiar bird costume ran across the sidewalk and collided with them. Everybody fell to the sidewalk, legs and wings and mouse heads and bird heads and girl heads and arms and bags a tangled mess.

"Mr. Beakman?" Laura got up and helped Trevor to his feet. She readily recognized Mr. Beakman's black feathers and huge yellow beak. "Can you help us? Is there any way to stop this thing from jerking Trevor around or at least slow it down?"

But the bird man just stared at her.

"Laura," Trevor said groggily. "Who are you talking to?"

"Mr. Beakman, please! There must be something."

The giant bird head tilted up and kept tilting up until it was almost straight up and down. Then the head fell open into two halves. At the very center, where the bird's wide throat should have been, was the head of a teenage boy.

Laura scrambled back a little in fear, half thinking that Mr. Beakman was a cannibal and had eaten someone. Then the boy blinked and said, "Sorry. I think you have me confused with someone else." The kid in the giant bird suit went his own way. Laura was at least thankful the collision stopped Trevor's head-on rush down the sidewalk.

As the night wore on she could see that the trick-or-treaters were now older on average. She couldn't be sure how accurate this impression was, since so many of them were completely covered in costumes and/or face paint, but if she looked at their relative size and the way they moved she didn't think she could be too far off. Laura also thought the costumes in general were more creative, more interesting, but also more disturbing. Some of the disguises would have been terrifying if she'd seen them out on the streets at any other time than Halloween. Halloween made the things she saw that evening less scary, because she could just tell herself it was someone in a costume, and although she could admire what they had done, it made it harder to be scared by it. And all those masks together, so many of them and so many so similar, they were just too familiar to terrify.

Like the giant roach that had just come out of the shadows by those trees—it was a great costume, all black and shiny and with that terrible bug face—it looked exactly like a nasty old roach, but only much bigger. And if she had run into it late one night in the middle of July she would absolutely freak out, no question. But seeing it on Halloween night, it was great, it was clever, but she probably wouldn't lose any sleep over it.

There were other costumes that just made her feel puzzled and uncomfortable, like they were part of some big joke she didn't understand. Just as she and Trevor were turning the corner from Lincoln Street onto Joliet Avenue they ran into five people walking together wearing exactly the same mask—a man's thin face with a curved chin and a giant nose. But each person wore a different outfit with that same mask, and one of them was a girl in a cheerleading outfit. What was *that* all about?

A few minutes later she saw an older guy—he must have been her dad's age for goodness sake—wearing a green mask with plants growing out of it—a little tree, a flower, some cacti, even a plant with some tomatoes hanging from it. What was he supposed to be—plant fertilizer?

Three kids in cat masks came jogging slowly by. As one, they turned their faces to stare at her, then simultaneously turned their faces away. Their legs were perfectly aligned as they moved, and they managed to move so slowly it was almost as if they were floating on magical cat feet.

The creepiest were the older teenagers in the simplest, plainest masks who never identified themselves or said anything—the ones who just stared. It would be one thing if Laura saw only one or two of those during the night—there would always be a few weirdos like that out at any event, but this Halloween she saw too many fitting that basic description. The teenagers stood around, motionless, staring at each other and the other trick-or-treaters who walked by. Except these teenagers weren't even trick-or-treating—they carried no bags or buckets or containers of any kind. And they didn't knock on people's doors. They just hung around on the corner and watched other people in costume go up to the houses and knock on doors. It was as if they were waiting for something big to happen.

Laura really didn't want to hang around to see what creepy event they were waiting for, so she hurried Trevor past them as fast as she could.

They encountered a kid in a bunny suit carrying a big alarm clock. "Does that clock tell real time?" she asked. He nodded proudly and showed them. Great. It wasn't at all what her goofy watch said, but they were doing fine on time.

The mouse head had pretty much behaved itself the past hour—occasionally snapping its mouth, occasionally licking inappropriately, but not much more. Trevor had only now and then spoken up from inside the mask to say that he was hungry, or thirsty, or tired. Laura tried to give him what he asked for, but she really didn't feel like she was helping him much.

"Want to know a secret?" Trevor asked abruptly.

She stopped and stared at him. This was the most he'd sounded like himself in some time.

"Only if you want to tell me."

"I've never really liked Halloween," he said.

"What? Trev, don't let this thing with the mask spoil it for you!"

"I always thought I was supposed to like it. *You* liked it. Dad likes it. I like the summer. But the fall and winter—it's like they get together and murder the summer every year and bury it in the back yard, under a bunch of dead leaves or under a bunch of snow."

Laura laughed. "Well, I guess in the old days that's kind of what they believed. The Irish people. *Samhain* came, and that meant the death of summer."

"Well, I don't like Sam Hane, then. He should leave summer alone. Everybody dresses up and they try to be scary, and they have parties and they eat so much candy it makes them sick, and it's all supposed to be fun, but it's all just pretending, isn't it? It's really just sad and it's about people being gone and not ever coming back."

Laura looked down then, thinking of Granddad. "Yeah, I know. It's about that, too."

"And they have Halloween *dances*!" he cried. "How

dumb is that? To dance about things that are scary and dead and *sad*."

Laura thought about it. "Sometimes people dance when they're sad. I think it's sorta traditional."

"Well, it bothers me and I don't *understand*. It *bothers* me."

"I know, Trev. I don't really understand either. Maybe when we're older, but I'm not sure that makes *that* much difference. I look at Mom and Dad, they help us with getting through this stuff, but I'm not sure they understand it much better than we do. I think part of being an adult is dealing with lots of things you don't really understand."

"Remember last year," Trevor said, "when Mom and Dad wouldn't let me go on that camping trip with Kenny and his parents because I hadn't been doing my chores?"

"Oh, I remember—you were so mad. You were mad for a *week*."

"I said to them 'I wish I was dead.' I said that to Mom and Dad."

Laura sighed. "I didn't know that."

"People shouldn't *say* stuff like that, Laura. They really *shouldn't*."

Who you love and who loves you? How does this happen and why? How can you be so here and tomorrow you're so gone? What do you do with a day, any day? And what does it mean? How can you be important, when every-thing feels so important, and nothing feels important at all? What is it that you feel, about anything?

"I believe I owe you a-a-an a—a-apology."

With a voice like that it could be no one else other than Dr. Blaack, but Laura couldn't see him. She was pretty sure the voice was coming from that shadow within the dark space between two buildings. There did appear to be movement there, and an area where the darkness was slightly grayer, as if something or someone were approaching. Then the area became clearer, and she could now see it was a cloud of frantically moving moths, hundreds of them.

"Hello Laura, dear," Doctor Blaack said directly into her ear. She twisted her head around nervously and saw that he was standing right beside her.

"Yii!" she yelled.

"Sorry, oh so s-s-sorry," he said. "I didn't mean to frighten you."

She stared up at him, so incredibly tall right beside her as he gazed down with his cow-like eyes from that height. His paintbrush-like goatee bobbed up and down like a very busy hairbrush. "I never intend to be so... mysterious, but whatever my intentions, that always appears to be the effect."

"Are you here to watch Trevor's mask drop off? Are you here to take it back to your shop?"

"Hmmm. Well, not precisely. Someone has not been completely forthcoming. Now, I assume full responsibility for not having initially told you that you could not tell anyone of young Trevor's predicament, including your very competent—I am sure—parents. But you must understand. What is the old saying? So many masks so little time? There are so many, including the dangerous ones, I cannot always readily recall their particular rules and restrictions."

"I guess that makes sense," she replied, "but it could have been a disaster."

"And still could be, I'm afraid."

"Wait, what do you mean?"

"As I said before, someone has not exactly been forthcoming." Doctor Blaack kept glancing off into the shadows, but she saw nothing there. "Someone did not tell you everything I instructed him to tell you."

"Wait! Are you saying my little brother is in even *more* danger?"

"Oh, there's still time, but not as much as—*oh bother*— Beakman! Beakman, come out here into the light and explain yourself!"

And inside those shadows which Laura could have sworn were empty a moment ago, except for maybe a tiny moth or two—the shiny tip of a yellow beak appeared, followed by the rest of it, and then those large, wet, sad Beakman eyes. He shuffled up beside his employer, beak weighing him down, eyes staring at his great big bird feet.

"Tell her, Beakman. Tell her what you purposely did not tell her before."

Beakman looked up, but would not meet Laura's eyes. "It wasn't on purpose—"

"Beakman!" Doctor Blaack thundered.

Poor Beakman's smallest feathers shook uncontrollably. Laura would have felt sorry for him except apparently he had withheld something he was supposed to tell her and that wasn't cool.

"I neglected to tell you," he continued, "that you must have your brother back at the mask shop before midnight strikes. Otherwise the mouse head will remain tightly fixed in place and cannot be removed."

"What? Why didn't you tell us?" Laura stepped closer. She was so mad she wanted to hit him. They'd wasted all this time!

"I—I'm not sure," Beakman replied. Doctor Blaack raised his hand menacingly and Beakman ducked his head in a panic. "All right, all right! I just thought maybe, maybe I could use a little company, a little help around the store. There's so much, you see—and if he was stuck inside the mask forever he would have to remain with us."

"True, true, there is a great deal—" Doctor Blaack interjected.

"And I get very lonely—I have been there since I was Trevor's age," Beakman said.

"Trevor's age!" Laura exclaimed. "But that must have been—"

"*Years* ago," Doctor Blaack said, interrupting. "Indeed he was just a boy when he first joined me."

Laura stared at Beakman, who shuffled his feet back and forth, and nodded and waved his wings around nervously. She thought she might actually attack him. But he was just like a little boy. A little boy in a man's, or rather great bird's, body.

"So," she said, looking at Doctor Blaack firmly. "The both of you, you've put my brother in danger. So take us to your shop *right now*! We'll wait until midnight, and then this nightmare will be *over*!"

"One would think that would be the logical thing of course," Doctor Blaack said, frowning. "But I'm afraid that's not how it works. He will have to return to the shop without my aid. But don't worry—there's plenty of time. I just wanted to make sure you *knew*, and that you did not stray far from the vicinity of available bus stops."

"We're going to find a bus right *now*," she said. "You

two just better *be there* when we get there. Could I have a time check?" she asked, but deliberately didn't say anything about the troubles with her watch. The last thing she needed was a panicky Trevor.

Doctor Blaack showed her his watch without comment.

"Okay, okay then—that's not so bad," she said, more for Trevor's benefit than anything else. She personally was terrified. Doctor Blaack was already in the process of leaving, fading back into the shadows behind him, Beakman at his side.

At the last moment Beakman turned around, squawked, "S-s-sorry!" and disappeared.

*M*rs. White had a fright
In the middle of the night
She saw a ghost eating toast
Halfway up a lamp post

So slow, so tired, and so slow when you're tired. Everybody else is having fun. Everybody else is laughing and joking and running around and eating themselves silly— well just let them! They can have their parties and their hungers and their bellyaches and their fun— all she wants is the paradise that is sleep.

Laura checked the bus schedule she had in her

pocket and figured out that the stop at 18th Avenue would get them to Doctor Blaack's in plenty of time to make the midnight deadline. They both had bus passes for the month so money wouldn't be a problem. What *was* a problem would be explaining to their parents *why* they were late and *where* they had *been* all that time. So they would get in serious trouble—right now that seemed like the least of their problems.

It was no time to relax—they were going to head over to that stop right *now* and wait for the bus to come. The mouse head had remained silent through all this; it appeared to have completely run out of steam. It had been quiet as a mouse, in fact—so much so that when they headed for the bus stop she wanted to make sure that Trevor was still safely tucked inside.

"Trevor, you in there?"

"Yeah, can we go home yet? I'm tired of trick-or-treating."

"We have to stay out til midnight, remember? That's when the mask comes off."

"Finally! I'm sick of this smelly old mask! It smells like—it smells like old mouse!"

"I know it does. One thing, though, we have to go back to Doctor Blaack's to make it happen."

"Laura! That's all the way downtown!"

"I know, Trev. But that's just the way it works. So you help me, okay? You help me get this silly mouse head down to Doctor Blaack's so we can get it off you, okay? We're going straight to the bus stop—*no detours!*"

He nodded wearily. She grabbed him by the hand to hurry him along. He resisted at first—he didn't like people holding his hand—but then she felt the hand relax inside hers. He'd given in.

They were on their way to this miraculous bus stop when they saw what looked to be a bunch of cardboard boxes and a few spilt bags of trash piled up against a lamp pole. Before Laura knew what was happening Trevor shook free of her hand and raced ahead of her and went down on his hands and knees by the boxes. The mouse head made loud snorting and sniffing noises.

Laura came up behind Trevor and grabbed him by the shoulders and tried to pull him off the sidewalk. "Trevor! We can't be *late!*" It was embarrassing and scary, seeing him out of control at such a crucial time. But the mouse head made Trevor a lot heavier than he used to be and she couldn't budge him.

Trevor was digging through the trash and within

seconds uncovered a pale, red-stained hand. "Ahhhhh!" Laura jumped back.

Trevor leaned over the hand and that pale tongue fell out onto the hand as he began licking it.

Something in the pile groaned and the trash started shifting. Laura jumped back (a little embarrassed since her little brother Trevor was right in there, but then, Trevor thought he was a mouse right now and she'd just never cared much for gross things thank-you-very-much). But as she watched the trash slide away, exposing more and more of the cardboard boxes underneath, the familiar parts of a robot began to reveal themselves. "Frank?" The cardboard boxes sat up shakily, the robot head weaving back and forth.

She put her hands on him to steady him. The cardboard pieces were a little greasy and she tried not to think about what it was her hands might be touching. "Frank, are you okay?"

The robot head looked up at her—there were holes covered with plastic where the eyes were, and although it was dark inside the robot head she was pretty sure she saw reflections from Frank's glasses. The box nodded. "Kind of," Frank's voice came out, muffled. "Some people knocked me down and dumped garbage on me.

I guess they didn't like my costume." She helped him get to his feet. Trevor helped too, in a sniffy, licky, mousy sort of way. "The weird thing was they all had the same mask on."

"Thin face, curved chin, giant nose?"

"That's the one," he said. "All but one of them had street clothes on and that mask. A funny thing, though, one of the girls was dressed in a cheerleader's uniform."

Laura got some clean pieces of newspaper and wiped the dirt and trash off his costume as best she could. The mouse head helped clean him up too—unfortunately by licking. She hoped Frank couldn't tell. "There. Almost as good as new. Almost," she said.

"I was on my way to the party. It's probably started by now. You're going aren't you?"

"Well, I wanted to, but I'm afraid I have to help Trevor with something very important. We can't be late."

"That's too bad. I was kind of hoping you guys would walk with me. Not that I'm afraid those people will come back or anything. I'd just like *your*—the company."

"Oh, they were probably just bored. They won't be back. I think you'll be okay. Frank, I really wanted to come with you."

"Does your brother *know* you have something you

have to do? Because he's headed toward the Flynn's, where the party is." She turned around and sure enough, there was Trevor walking very fast away from them. Although walking might be the wrong word. He was scrambling along with his head down and torso bent over, like some kind of animal. He was following some other kids into a well-lit house halfway down the block.

"There's no *time* for this! We have to *stop* him!"

She began running after him. Her beautiful mask kept slipping down and making it hard to see so she took it off and threw it away. After maybe a minute she heard Frank pounding the concrete behind her.

They stopped when they got onto the porch because of the crowd filling the doorway in front of them. Trevor had already gone inside. Laura pumped her knees up and down in frustration and pushed a little on the back of the kid in front of her—she just *had* to get Trevor out of there.

"Do I smell too bad now to get in?" Frank asked. "Because of all that trash I was in. Be *honest*, I don't want to embarrass myself."

She couldn't believe he was asking her such a question, but then Frank had *no idea* what was going on. "I don't think so," she said quickly. "I mean, there is a *smell*, but it's so faint. So unless you were really expecting it I don't see how you'd notice it. Besides, this place will be packed with dozens of kids sweating inside their hot, uncomfortable costumes. I seriously doubt yours will be the *worst* smell."

"Oh. Well thanks. I guess."

She may have hurt his feelings, but she couldn't worry about that right now. She pushed some more and people started complaining, but as soon as there was a small gap by the door she squeezed through leaving Frank behind. A wall of sound and light and yes, body stink, hit her in the face. And *heat*. It was *amazing* the amount of heat a bunch of kids could generate in a small space, maybe enough to heat a house like this for an entire winter.

Some people in town would probably think the world was really going downhill if they saw this party. There were cats dancing with dogs and even—oh my!— *lobsters*, aliens shaking their *booties* with black swans and Air Force captains in close conversation with decaying red-eyed zombies.

But no mouse heads as far as she could see. *Where was Trevor?* "Trevor!" she shouted, but in all the noise he obviously wouldn't be able to hear her. She looked around for some adults.

The Flynns were off in one corner with the punch bowl and the turntable. Mrs. Flynn was dressed in a witch costume with a tall cone-shaped hat, but she also had these delicate little fairy wings strapped to her shoulder, so maybe she was either a fairy witch or a witch fairy. She was laughing loudly—about as loudly as the very loud music—and passing around cups of punch and pumpkin cookies to anybody with a hand out.

Mr. Flynn stood behind the sound system in an expensive looking vampire outfit that was all red and white silk and shiny black cloth and the collar of his cape was even taller than his head, which actually made him look more ridiculous than sinister. Shiny white plastic vampire fangs kept popping out of his mouth when he talked. He was talking animatedly to a girl standing beside him. It was Tammy.

Tammy still had on that "Property of the County Jail" shirt she'd worn to school. She held a couple of CDs in her hand. She looked pretty excited and happy. Laura guessed it was her choosing the music. It was that driving, bumpy, heavy-on-the-bass music they always played at parties—not that she'd been to that many parties, but that was what she'd always heard.

"So do you like the music?" Frank said beside her. He'd caught up to her. She smiled at him nervously. She guessed this was his serious attempt to make conversation. But she really had *no* time for this. She regretted that she was probably going to have to hurt his feelings again. The first time a boy had ever shown interest in her, but at the *absolutely worst* time.

"It's nice," she said rapidly. "It has a good beat I guess. Can you help me find my little brother? We *really* have to *go!*"

"Sure, I—" but she was already pushing her way across the room looking for Trevor. She didn't have time to listen to his answer. "It's *techno!*" he shouted after her.

The room was suddenly much more crowded as the music became faster and more people started dancing. Laura was panicky. How was she going to find a mouse head in this crowd?

Suddenly someone grabbed her hand and pulled her out of the crowd. It was Roger from school, an older boy she'd never even talked to before. "Hey girl, let's *dance!*" Laura felt her face blush as she realized she had no idea what to do. She used to fantasize about going to dances, but this was *awful*. What if they were *too late* getting back to Doctor Blaack's? She tried to pull her hand away but Roger held on tightly.

"I *can't*!" she shouted.

"Come on, now! Don't be *shy*!"

"I have to find *my brother*!"

Something boxy came up behind Roger and put its hand on his shoulder and pulled him away. "You heard her!" the robot shouted. It was Frank. She had just a second to think how great that was when she lost her balance and fell into the crowd behind her. She was grabbing on to anything she could get her hands on to stay upright.

"Get off of me!" Someone—a giant *squirrel*?—shouted and squirmed away, and she fell on the floor.

Several guys had come to the party dressed in jeans and a hoody and wearing some sort of generic rubber "ghoul" mask tucked inside the hoody. She saw those kinds of masks every year—they were from some movie she hadn't been allowed to see. They stood above her now, all four or five of them, completely silent, looking down and staring at her. It totally creeped her out.

Then a small kid in a gray wig and a long gray beard pushed forward between their legs and bent over her. She recognized him because of his baby face. Joe Thompson, the youngest kid in their class. In that old man outfit he looked too weird for words. "You *fell!*" he said, pointing and laughing. *Such a dweeb.*

But then suddenly Frank appeared and stretched out his hand and pulled her up. She started to thank him when there was a loud explosion of alarm from one of the other rooms, and she suddenly felt both excited and frightened. Could all that commotion be because of Trevor?

"*Gather you spooks and gather you demons, gather you werewolves, mermaids, and clowns. Watch all your pets and shelter all your babies, for monster and mouse have come to your town!*"

Kids were streaming out of that room crying and drenched in water. Some of them had their hands tied behind their backs! Laura struggled to get closer but the crowd kept pushing her back. Someone put a wet hand on her arm and it felt as if she'd been burned. But when she checked her arm all she found was a cold, wet patch of skin and goosebumps.

Suddenly Frank grabbed her arm and pulled her to the side away from that stream of running kids. "This way!" he yelled, and pulled her into the less-crowded dining room. "There's a side exit to the yard!"

"No!" she cried. "My brother's probably in there. I have to grab him! If we don't leave *soon* we're going to be *late*!"

"This way then," he said, "There's another entrance on the other side of that room!" and guided her along with him against the wall. She noticed that his costume was in pretty bad shape—the cardboard dented and torn in numerous places, the carefully painted electronic designs smeared, many of the little dials and electrical decorations he'd glued on ripped off completely or dangling. More pieces fell off as they scraped against the wall, exposing part of his arm, part of a shoulder, several sections of the white T-shirt he was wearing underneath.

Laura could feel her alarm rising like a rapidly worsening fever. She had no idea what caused the mass hysterical exit from the other room or all that water—had someone turned a hose on those kids?

She should have been holding on to Trevor's hand the whole time. She shouldn't have turned her head away for even a *moment*. Now she knew a little about what moms with little kids went through—you had to watch those crazy kids every second! She should have just held on to him until they'd reached the bus stop. Whatever it took. She should have taken care of her little brother.

Frank was first through the door into the other room. By that time most everybody else was out of the way and back in the kitchen or outside. She could hear Mr. Flynn somewhere, his voice raised, frantically trying to find out what happened.

"Is that your little brother?" Frank asked ahead of her, sounding amazed.

She pushed past—what was left of Frank's cardboard robot costume was so fragile it fell off as she brushed against him. She gazed around the room. Water was everywhere, in puddles all over the floor and splashed up on the walls. Bright, wet red apples were scattered over the soaked rug, many of them chewed or with big bites missing. Large old-fashioned galvanized metal washtubs had been place around the room, about half of them empty, turned on their sides or upside down.

A torn banner still half-hanging from the ceiling explained that this was the "Apple Bobbing" competition. Trevor was standing in the middle of one of those metal tubs, soaked and shivering.

The mouse head stared at her with huge, coal dark eyes. Wet, the head looked smaller than it had before, skinnier, like a drowned rat. Had that comparison ever been more correct? It also looked furious, dripping water into the washtub and onto the floor. Its cheeks were sunken, its neck damp and matted.

Trevor bent at the knees, as if he were about to pass out. His shoulders looked thin and pointy. This was still Trevor's body, of course, but it was so wet his jeans and long-sleeved shirt looked darker, more ragged, kind of like a furry suit. Like he was turning completely into a mouse.

"Trevor?" she could hear her voice shaking. The mouse head tilted, those terrible dark eyes examining her. The mouse head's mouth opened and made a chilling and painful rasping noise. Then without warning Trevor's body leapt out of the tub, shook itself off, splattering water all over her face, and raced past her. "Trevor!"

"Can I help?" Frank asked.

For a second she actually forgot why Frank was there. Then she grabbed his hand. "You're sweet." She made herself smile. "But he's my brother. He might hurt you."

She ran into the living room and saw Trevor's back as he dashed out the front door. He was still dripping water everywhere. Mr. and Mrs. Flynn were standing there talking to Tammy. They all three stared at her.

"I'm really sorry," she said. "I—my family—we'll pay for any damages." Then she raced out the door after him.

Once outside, Laura saw that Trevor was a good ten yards ahead of her. He wasn't exactly running, more like scrambling on all fours, but moving fast enough to maintain his distance. "Trevor, please!" she called. "We *have* to get to that bus stop!" But he didn't slow down. Now and then he would look over his shoulder at her, dark eyes blinking, but if he actually recognized who she was he didn't act like it, and he didn't say a word no matter how much she pleaded. If she sped up, so did he. He could have gotten far ahead of her, to the point where she'd lose sight of him completely, but he never let that happen either. This was all her fault, and she had no idea how to fix it.

Trevor/mouse led her through a series of alleys and across open lots, behind the streets she knew, then behind streets she had never heard of before. Eventually the skyline made from moonlight and streetlight peeping above and around the dark buildings was the skyline of some strange new place she had never seen before, a place perhaps only a mouse would know, smelling of sugar maples and sweet grasses and berry bushes. These berry bushes were now brown and broken, lying on the ground, but a mouse knows how to get food even out of dead things.

Laura gradually became aware of a faint rotting smell. There were great piles of dead leaves still around, huge piles that people hadn't yet gotten around to spreading on their garden or burning in their incinerators. Burning leaves was only permissible on certain days because of air pollution. It was hard to think of their nice, clean town as being polluted but pollution was pretty much everywhere these days. People didn't always notice because they were just so used to it, which was kind of sad.

Her dad really hated it when people didn't take care of their leaves. It was one of the few things that annoyed him. The leaves soaked up the rain water and animals would crawl in there and die and after a while the leaf piles smelled sour and a little longer after that they started smelling rotten.

But this smell was even worse than that. This was just an all-around really intense, really bad dead smell.

Thinking of their parents brought her to the edge of tears. Surely they would have known what she should do, if only she could tell them about this. How would she explain it to them if anything happened to Trevor?

Eventually she followed Trevor and the mouse head through another empty field and out another alley into a neighborhood very similar to her own. There were porches and sidewalks and lots of trees and jack-o'-lanterns with their glowing eyes and burning smiles like watchmen in front of each house. And down at the end of the sidewalk she saw a tall figure with bandaged arms and a face hidden from view.

The mouse head raised its snout and sniffed the air. It turned—its fur now dry and fluffy and full—and gazed at her. Then Trevor/mouse took off scampering between two houses. She followed breathlessly, positive now they would be too late for the bus and too late for Trevor to lose the mask, but she needed to be with him and help him in any way she could.

They went between the houses and came out into another neighborhood that was much the same and yet vaguely different in its details. Surely it was close to midnight, but when Laura looked at her watch it was still broken, the hands spinning crazily so she really had no idea of the time. Laura hadn't seen any trick-or-treaters in a while and most of the pumpkins on the porches of the houses on this street had lost their glow and gray smoke floated up from their mouths like some kind of ghostly conversation.

But out in the middle of the street a little boy in dark clothes sat astride a dark little bicycle. She couldn't see his face and she couldn't see his hands and when he pedaled the bicycle all she could see of his bike was its whirling shadow. Then the little boy started making snarly sounds like some kind of beast. His bike was like a silent ship sailing over the road and then over the sidewalk as he made his way toward them. She wanted to run away so badly but she couldn't leave Trevor.

The mouse head turned and looked at her again.

"I'm still here, Trev! I'm going to stay with you no matter what and no matter how long it takes!" Trevor/mouse turned back around and ran through a driveway into even more darkness. And Laura followed.

They came out into yet another neighborhood that again looked almost the same but somehow different in its details. The pumpkins on the porches were dead and flat and she could smell the rot of them even from the street. But that didn't make sense—it was way too soon. It was still Halloween night.

Near the middle of this block there was a dilapidated house with a sagging roof and drooping windows and a wide, lopsided door. Laura watched as the door eased open. The wind on this street made a sound like some kind of wild animal and all the leaves and dust and trash trapped inside the gust gave it a kind of physical body. It looked like the shadow of a giant lion, or a tiger, or a bear. Whatever it was, this giant wind animal rushed inside the house and the door slammed shut trapping it inside. The wind animal roared and shook the house and then whimpered as if begging to be set free. It shook the walls so that the whole house shimmered as if it were about to disappear, but still the house would not let it go.

Laura had always dreamed that there were houses like that. Sad houses and vengeful houses that would not let you go. And sometimes a house could be like this giant mask you not only wore over your head, but over your entire life. There was a house on the next block of her neighborhood where really terrible things happened to the children who lived there. They hadn't given many details in the paper, but it had been enough to help her imagine the rest, although she figured there had to have been things that had been so bad she couldn't even imagine them. But every time she'd passed that house she thought how tired it looked, how everything that happened inside it had been all too much for it to handle.

But finally some construction company bought it and gave it a completely new face, a completely different mask, and the mask had been a good thing because it was never that tired old house again.

Laura wasn't really afraid of ghosts and goblins and werewolves and vampires. She was afraid of some other people, because people were capable of doing the worst, the most awful things she couldn't even imagine.

To Laura's surprise this ghastly path was the street Trevor/mouse decided to go down. He hustled past the house full of wind, and he hustled past a tree full of burned out jack-o'-lanterns sitting on the branches. The jack-o'-lanterns fell to the ground like overripe fruit one after the other as he passed. He walked past a lonely gray house with a kid's sad plastic swimming pool sitting on the front lawn.

For some reason Laura felt the need to walk up onto the lawn of this fading gray house—she couldn't help herself. She found dozens of discarded masks lying on the ground like leaves fallen from a mask tree, and several more masks face down in the swimming pool full of water and candy wrappers and an old brown treat bag.

They passed another house with a rocking chair on the front porch and she saw someone in the rocking chair watching her but she couldn't see the face of that person and she was very uncomfortable about that.

She stopped and gazed defiantly at the figure on the porch, waiting for it to rock, but the figure in the chair remained still. Then the tree branches moved and allowed some more moonlight to slip by and she realized then that the figure was some kind of dummy. Still, she would have liked some kind of polite response.

At the next house there was an old man in a window who moved like a puppet. Then Laura realized he actually was a puppet.

Trevor/mouse came to the very end of this street and stopped at the bus stop. Laura held her breath. She really had no idea where they were, or where a bus from this stop might take them. Not that it mattered much anyway—it was obviously well past midnight and too late for Trevor to escape that awful mouse head. She looked at her watch once again. The hands were still spinning, so fast now they were a blur. It was all her fault. Why had she let him get away from her?

Why hadn't she gotten another watch, or at least told Doctor Blaack hers had gone crazy? The stakes had been so very high and she'd done everything wrong and now her little brother was going to have to pay the price.

An old bus pulled up to the stop silently and opened its doors. It was battered, rusty, and ancient—she couldn't believe the city would still run a bus in this kind of shape. With its round headlights and the fierce-looking chrome front grill, the chipped pale green and light yellow paint job and the old-fashioned lettering, the bus looked like a prop from an old movie or from one of those ads in an old Life magazine like they had at the library.

But the sign above the windshield said "Downtown" and Trevor/mouse scampered aboard on all fours like an animal. Did the age of the bus really make that much difference? It was the only choice they had. The driver's face was invisible, completely hidden in shadow. "So you're bringing a pet?" He nodded toward Trevor/mouse. "I'll still have to charge you for its fare. Cash or bus pass?" She flashed both her card and Trevor's and the driver nodded. "So sit down."

"Excuse me. Could you give me the time?"

"Half hour until midnight, little lady," he replied, and started up the bus.

She was shocked it was still that early, but it didn't help them. Their first trip down to the mask shop had taken much longer than that.

Trevor/mouse grabbed an aisle seat about midway back. He didn't look at her but kept his dark eyes fixed ahead. She took a seat one row ahead of him, thinking she could box him in if he tried to escape.

So they'd go back to Doctor Blaack's anyway, even if it was too late. She could at least stay with Trev a while if he was going to become part of their permanent staff. Just like Beakman. Maybe Doctor Blaack had some alternatives he could make work. Maybe she could even exchange places with Trevor, or serve part of his time. In any case Doctor Blaack probably had some sort of advice about what they should do, or how she could tell her parents what she had done.

Laura used to think sometimes that she was all ready to be an adult. After all, what more was there to know? But it was all about knowing how things worked, what to expect and what the secret rules might be. Or even what the real questions were. Or what to do in an emergency like when your brother turns into a giant mouse. She guessed those were the things adults figured out through experience.

Of course Trevor/mouse knew she was there—they were on the same bus after all—but it acted like she was invisible. It ignored her, not once looking back or in any other way showing an interest. But then why did it wait for her except to make sure they got on the same bus together? That's what reassured Laura that Trevor was still in there somewhere, that he still had some influence over what the mouse head did with his body. He still needed her to be close, and Laura was determined not to let him down.

At this time of night all the trick-or-treaters were safe at home in their beds, probably having weird dreams because of all the candy they had eaten. But she doubted any were having a dream weirder than this.

There were still people out in costume, besides her (although she had lost most of it) and Trevor. Mostly older, mostly different, and they were wearing the costumes like they had to, not like they wanted to. At first she thought she and Trevor had boarded an empty bus, but there were one or two more, including an older fellow a couple of rows ahead of her—he had wrinkles on his hands and forearms. But he wore a large paper bag over his head with a couple of little holes poked out—maybe with his fingers—for his eyes to see through, and a larger hole torn out for his mouth that was all wet from his lips and his tongue. The brown paper around the hole was almost transparent and falling away in chunks. It was weird. Maybe he was a little crazy—crazy people rode the bus all the time. But for some reason she thought he was probably harmless.

He'd drawn some eyebrows on with red crayon and a big nose that he had colored blue. From time to time he made a sighing sound, like he was very tired, or very sad.

Every few blocks they'd pass an adult in costume walking down the sidewalk in the dark or standing on the edge of the street doing nothing, just watching the few cars and trucks that drove by at this time of night.

Sometimes the walkers just had a simple plastic mask on, and sometimes just a piece of paper or cardboard with a face drawn on it or holes cut in it, like the man on the bus with the paper bag. They held these drawings up to their faces when they saw people, or they taped them to a hat, or maybe their forehead, to keep them more or less in place. She couldn't imagine it was fun for them. It was more like they felt obligated.

A few of the people out on the street had these old homemade papier-mâché masks on, like the ones the kids had worn at school when they were pretending to be ancient Celts, but even cruder than those, falling apart, falling off their faces, with words and symbols drawn on them with lipstick and magic marker. In their own way they were scarier than any store-bought mask she'd ever seen.

The old bus rocked back and forth as it picked up speed. Laura held on to the seatback in front of her. On the wider curves she slid scarily across the seat. No one said anything and the bus never stopped. Trevor/mouse still sat calmly but Laura felt anything but calm.

Then with a loud clank and a jerk that almost sent Laura tumbling out into the aisle the bus stopped abruptly with a grind and a squeal. "All out!" the bus driver's staticky voice announced on the loud speaker. Then he turned around and looked down the aisle and said conversationally, "Folks, we're downtown." Laura felt relieved.

Trevor/mouse got up immediately and filed out with the others. Laura struggled to catch up but she felt suddenly so exhausted she had to steady herself by clutching the seat backs with each step she made. When she came alongside the driver she said politely, "Thank you. How did you get here so quickly?"

The driver looked at her in surprise and said, "Ma'am, didn't you know you were on the express?"

Chicken my chicken my creamy crow,
I went to the well to wash my toe,
When I got there the water was low,
What time is it, Old Witch, Old Witch?
What time is it Old Witch?

Thankfully Trevor/mouse had waited for her at the bottom of the steps. He seemed nervous and ready to go. "Come on Trevor!" Laura started running in the direction of Dr. Blaack's Mask Shop, Trevor/mouse running alongside of her. Despite the circumstances it was almost fun. The streets downtown were much darker than before. Many of the shop lights and some of the street lights had been turned off. Trevor/mouse had pulled slightly ahead of her, very focused, not looking back anymore to make sure she kept pace. Because of the darkness it was sometimes hard to avoid obstacles. She'd knock over a trash can or bump her knee against a short post. She knew she'd be really sore in the morning but she kept running anyway as fast as she could.

Mouse parts or not, Laura had much longer legs than Trevor, and soon had pulled up alongside him again. He glanced over at her and she could see the Trevor eyes inside the wide deep eye-holes of the mask—tired and weepy and scared all at the same time—but at least he was still in there.

"Laura! We're running so *fast*!" Trevor yelled. And she recognized even more of his face inside that mouse head. It seemed as if maybe Trevor had gotten a little more control over his body for this last dash toward the shop. The mouse head probably didn't care. The mouse head was fine with the way things were, comfortable in its mouse thoughts and hungers forever.

But Trevor didn't have the strength, or the animal fierceness of the mouse head—Trevor was just a little boy—and Laura worried he might not have it in him to get back into Doctor Blaack's in time.

But he was trying and Laura cheered him on. "Come on, Trev," she said. "You're almost there," she repeated, again and again. His eyes rolled past the eyeholes like little animals hunted by some terrible predator, but he was still trying. He did everything he could.

They reached the empty storefront beside Doctor Blaack's, running so fast and so hard Laura was afraid they might crash through the window. Their hands slapped the dusty glass and Laura swore she saw figures inside scattering into some shadowy corner of that vacant building.

At last they stood in front of Doctor Blaack's, whose interior was dark except for a flickering blue fluorescent bulb in the front display window bathing the merchandise inside. It amazed Laura that here at the end of Halloween there appeared to be many more masks in this window than there had been the last time they'd been here. Hundreds of masks were piled into the window, but instead of being attractively displayed it really looked as if they'd just been dumped there, as if the display window was just some glass-walled storage box for storing a large quantity of masks. Some were upside down and sideways and however they'd landed after being tossed inside.

Laura didn't know exactly what she'd expected, maybe not a wide open door with people blowing trumpets as they entered but certainly something more than this. They knew they were coming, didn't they, or was the problem that they'd never really expected Trevor and Laura to make it here on time?

Laura started banging on the door. "Doctor Blaack! Let us in—it's almost midnight!"

Trevor pointed with an unsteady hand. Laura looked and saw the little card—*After Hours Buzzer*—posted above a worn, cream-colored button. She pushed it as hard as she could, then she pushed it again. Off in the distance—it sounded miles away—she heard a faint buzzing, like a bee trapped deep inside an underground hive.

There was a click, and the door creaked open a few inches. They both pushed their way inside.

"Doctor Blaack! Doctor Blaack!" she cried. Still no answer. She was furious after all they'd been through. With Doctor Blaack, with Beakman, with Halloween. "C'mon, Trev—I bet we're supposed to go to the backroom. That's where you put it on—I bet that's where you're supposed to take it off."

But Trevor didn't answer. She looked around, and there he was, crouching down, his mouse head sleeker, wilder looking, as he fell to all fours. "Trevor!"

The mouse head snarled, showing a mouth full of huge teeth, and took off, running just like, like a giant mouse!

Laura stared after him in shock. Beside her, a huge cat's head mask with blood red eyes opened its mouth and said, "Time won't wait!"

"Trevor!" she called.

"Time won't wait!" said another mask and then another.

She'd seen the look in Trevor's eyes as he dropped to the floor and knew there was no reasoning with him. It was the mouse that wanted to keep his body and it was the mouse that was now in *charge* of that body. She ran to another aisle, scanning as far as she could see into the store, searching for him.

A gorilla's face hanging at the beginning of the next aisle suddenly became animated, blinked several times and growled out, "Time won't wait."

She thought she saw a glimpse of gray fur flashing

across the next aisle: thin chest and swollen upper legs, long muscular feet with claw-ended toes, dull beady eyes. "Time won't wait! Time won't wait!" cascaded down to her from mask after mask.

She glimpsed bits of shiny black and yellow between the costumes, over her head, against the back wall. "Beakman!" Finally Beakman stopped and stared at her, and then took off again as Trevor/mouse raced past and Beakman pursued.

"Time won't wait! Time won't wait!" came from every aisle, from the back, the front, the sides.

In the next aisle Trevor/mouse came straight at her, its head down and almost scraping the floor, its eyes glaring at her, shiny and mean. "Time won't wait!" said the pretty princess mask a few feet away in a deep, bass voice.

Laura screamed and waved her hands and tried to make herself look big. She'd heard that was what you were supposed to do if you came across a bear in the woods so why wouldn't it work with a mouse, even a giant one? To her relief Trevor/mouse turned and ran back the other way.

"Time won't wait!" the Pinocchio head said, its nose growing. Beakman appeared around the corner at the other end of the aisle, his great black wings stretched out and flapping loudly, herding Trevor/mouse back to the back wall, by the giant cash register. "Time won't wait! Time won't wait! Time won't wait!"

Laura ran down the aisle between lines of masks tormenting her, "Time!" flapping their mechanical mask jaws at her, "Won't!" and rolling their big buggy eyes, "Wait!" She followed Trevor/mouse and Beakman into the back room as every mask in the store appeared to be thundering at her like a broken record set on maximum volume, "Won't! Won't! Won't! Won't! Won't!"

She saw Doctor Blaack standing in the room observing everything. Beakman knocked Trevor down and sat on his chest. Doctor Blaack crouched down next to them and appeared to be giving Beakman instructions. "Don't hurt him!" she cried, ran over and grabbed Beakman's greasy feathered shoulder and tried to pull him off her brother.

"It's not c-c-coming off!" Doctor Blaack shouted from his squatting position beside Trevor's head. "The mouse won't le-e-e-et go!"

Laura climbed off Beakman and scrambled to the other side of the mouse head. Doctor Blaack was bent over and straining to pry off the mouse head. She couldn't help but notice the little bit of elastic at the back of Doctor Blaack's neck that had come undone, and how the skin around his neck appeared loose, and she had to wonder—was Doctor Blaack wearing a mask?

She kneeled down beside Trevor and slipped the tips of her fingers under the edges of the mouse head. Tiny bits of his skin were peeling off and wiggling around her fingertips. She shrieked and let go.

"Hurry—we only ha-a-a-ave seconds!" Doctor Blaack shouted.

She bent down close to Trevor's neck and noticed that there were dozens of pale, wiggling pink worm ends coming out of the edges of the mask and clutching Trevor's skin, hair, and clothing. Dozens of tiny mouse fingers and mouse toes. She pulled a nail file out of her back pocket. Her mother had given it to her months ago saying, "Keep this handy. You're almost a young woman. Some day you will want to use this." But she'd never even thought of using it until now.

She leaned over Trevor and used the nail file to saw back and forth across all those miniature toes and fingers.

The mouse head wrinkled its snout and burst into laughter, its tongue rolling and unrolling like one of those paper blowout squeaker party horns. Then it started to scream.

The mouse mask made a popping noise and flew off Trevor's face. Trevor blinked and stared up at Laura in confusion. He had rings and lines of sweaty dirt around his neck, down his cheeks, across his forehead, and under his eyes.

And oh how he stank!

B eakman drove them home in a bright yellow cab. Doctor Blaack sat in the front passenger seat.

Except it wasn't really a yellow cab. It was actually a beat up old gray station wagon with a giant yellow cab mask slipped over the front of it. You could even see where it was tied on. From the back it still looked like that battered old gray wagon. Like most things, it was two very different things at the same time.

Laura was furious with both Beakman and Doctor Blaack, the way they'd jerked her and her brother around, the danger they'd put them in. She was mad at Trevor, too. If he hadn't gone where he wasn't allowed they would never have had to go through this terrible ordeal.

But she couldn't hold on to that anger. It was really frustrating, because she really *wanted to be angry*. But she was just too relieved for that. They were almost home, and they were *safe*.

Doctor Blaack murmured to Beakman. "Beakman, you do have your *license* don't you?" He paused. Then, "Wha-a-at do you *mean* you're too *young*?" He twisted around and gazed at Trevor and Laura. "Are you feeling better, children? More rested?" They nodded. "Go-o-o-d! And I do hope you'll forgive me. Apparently due to Beakman's lack of responsibility I have involved you in a somewhat unusual, perhaps illegal circumstance."

"That's okay, Doctor Blaack," Laura replied unconvincingly. "We're almost home." She stared at his face, or his mask, whatever it was. She thought about asking him. But did not.

It was darker than dark outside, but the moon was full, and although she did not recognize these streets as her neighborhood of the daytime, she did recognize them as the neighborhood of her dreams.

Finally they drifted silently up to a small house with a big front yard and halted.

"Look, Laura, there's jack-o'-lanterns on our porch," Trevor said. "We didn't carve jack-o'-lanterns this year, did we?"

"No, no Trev. We got too busy with… other things. I guess Mom and Dad made them and put them up."

"Yeah," he replied. "I guess so. Look, there's a dad pumpkin, and a mom, and a really small one, and one just a little bit bigger. I bet those last two are supposed to be us!"

"I bet you're right."

Trevor stared at the jack-o'-lanterns for a while without getting out of the car. Laura didn't make any attempt to get out either. They were just so very tired.

"The lights are all gone out of our pumpkins. But there's a light on in the living room. Do you think that's Dad?" he asked softly. "Do you think he waited up for us?"

"I know he did," she replied. "Probably both of them are sitting there, waiting."

"Do you think they'll let us re-light the pumpkins so we can see what their smiles look like before we go to bed?"

"I don't think so, Trev. I think they're going to be *way* too mad."

"*What* are we going to tell them? Are we going to tell them the truth?"

"You should always tell the truth, Trev. Unless it's *way* too crazy. If it's way too crazy, well, then they think *you're* crazy."

"So what do we tell them?"

"You let me do the talking. I'm going to tell them I was irresponsible. *You* wanted to come home. *I* wanted to go to that party. You fell asleep, and I lost track of the time."

"You're going to be in a lot of trouble, Laura."

"*Absolutely.* But I'm okay with that. A small price to pay."

"B-b-before you go," Doctor Blaack said from the front seat. He handed her a mask. It was an adult woman's face but beautifully ornamented with flowers and curlicues and little dancing figures. A real work of art. "To replace the one you lost," he explained.

"Um, pretty," she said nervously. "But what does it... *do*?"

"A-a-absolutely *nothing*," he replied. "It's *just* pretty."

"Thanks!"

They climbed out of the car then, and walked up the sidewalk toward home without saying goodbye. After they were safely inside the house the darkened car pulled away from the curb and drove into the shadows.

Steve Rasnic Tem is the author of over 400 short stories and 7 novels and is a past winner of the Bram Stoker, British Fantasy, and World Fantasy awards. A collection of his selected stories, *Figures Unseen*, recently came out from Valancourt Books. His stories for children and young adults have appeared in such anthologies as *A Nightmare's Dozen*, edited by Michael Stearns, *Bruce Coville's Book of Spine-Tinglers 2*, and *Scary Out There*, edited by Jonathan Maberry.